YAXLEY'S CAT

Also by ROBERT WESTALL

Blitzcat
Ghost Abbey
The Promise

YAXLEY'S CAT

Robert Westall

**SCHOLASTIC
HARDCOVER**

Scholastic Inc.
New York

Library of Congress Cataloging-in-Publication Data

Westall, Robert.
Yaxley's cat / Robert Westall.
p. cm.
Summary: After Yaxley disappears, the inhabitants of an English village
fear that his ugly old cat will uncover the truth about the secret they are
hiding.

ISBN 0-590-45175-8

[1. Cats — Fiction. 2. Mystery and detective stories. 3. England —
Fiction.] I. Title.
PZ7.W51953Yax 1992
[Fic] — dc20   91-18341
                                                                       CIP
                                                                        AC

12 11 10 9 8 7 6 5 4 3 2 1   2 3 4 5 6 7/9

Printed in the U.S.A.   37

First Scholastic printing, April 1992

For Laura,
who experienced the cat
and gave me the idea

YAXLEY'S CAT

One

Rose found the coast of Norfolk very different from the coast of Suffolk.

In Suffolk, around Dunwich, the sea was eating the coast away. The soil cliffs crumbled, exposing tall slender mysterious towers of stone, which turned out to be medieval wells. The children, warned the cliffs were dangerous, still climbed looking for treasure. Timothy had found a vertebra, which he swore was human. It watched Rose beadily from the back shelf of the car. Till an old man in Southwold told her it was only a calf's vertebra; from a midden, not a grave. Whereupon she felt strong enough to ignore it.

Dunwich was a land of fable, like Lyonesse. Once the fourth city of England! Seventeen churches overwhelmed by the sea since the Middle Ages, and local legend said you could still hear their bells tolling under water, on stormy nights.

The old man at Southwold said the inhabitants

of Dunwich would tell you any lie; even that a ship full of pianos was torpedoed there in the war, and that on stormy nights the mermaids still sat playing them . . .

But in spite of his sarcasm, and the spookiness, Rose had liked the place. Dunwich was *impending*. Anything might happen at any time. The sea was a huge foggy roaring archaeologist, an angel of the Second Coming, when the secrets of all hearts would be revealed. At the moment, Rose would almost have welcomed a Second Coming; if only the secrets of her muddled heart *could* be revealed!

But in Norfolk, around Cley-next-the-Sea, she found the sea, perversely, was building the land up. The sea, which had always soothed her angry heart, was going away from her, giving up. The village, as if desperate to live up to its name, stretched like a thirsty despairing animal more than a mile from the roofless aisles of its medieval church, and still could no longer reach the sea. Its last gasp was a windmill with white sails and a red pantiled roof. For all its carefully nurtured beauty, it had the forlorn air of a traveller who had missed the last bus. Beyond stretched the grey flat foggy infinity of the salt-marshes. The sea was nowhere to be seen without a long muddy walk, and she had neither the heart nor the energy to go looking for her salty friend. Here, the secrets of no hearts would be revealed. No resurrection, but a muddy burial, layer on layer. Nothing would ever happen here again, except the waves would cease even to be heard, and the fishermen cease to fish.

2

She despaired, and wanted to go. But the children, like dogs, needed a walk, a sniff around, a *nosy*, as they called it. Or they would cease to be reasonable, and become unbearable.

So they went to find the sea, down the grey endless path. The children kept finding strange objects and fetching them back, like retrievers. Except the objects today seemed singularly damp and unsavoury. The squashed body of a frog, flat as a pancake, but still with the grimace of death on its face. A small fish, all staring eyes, stripped backbone, and tail. But one mustn't discourage the children. They had been taught to be curious; expected their questions answered. That, she and Philip had agreed on from the beginning. It was one of the few things they still agreed about.

She wondered how much the children guessed. They had been told it was a holiday, but it was really a flight, a flight from Philip. She had to get away, before the balloon really went up, before she began yelling and he put that irrevocably understanding look on his face. Philip did not like rows; he undermined her with reasonableness, trapped her angry wasp-buzzing with strands of logic, like a patient spider. Till she was unable to say anything; just scream inside.

Her mother said she was a fool. Mother lapped up Philip's flattery, couldn't get enough of Philip. Philip was handsome; his designer glasses just made him look even more intelligent than he was. Philip was tall and as fit and lean as a low-cholesterol diet and lots of squash could make him. Philip was successful; they had just relocated to a five-bedroom house; with plastic Ionic columns round the door, and most of the front garden taken up with two tarmaced driveways, one marked "In" and the other "Out." Well, it was logical, wasn't it? Just as logical as relocating when the housing market was falling. And so easy, relocating. Not like *moving* when you had to show dozens of interesting people round your house, and had marvellous back-breaking packing-up days, when you found stuff you thought you'd lost years ago. No back-break now. Men came and did everything, while you went for a long lunch at a hotel. Except, without the crises, was it *real*?

With Philip, was *anything* real any more? She had had a vague misty dream of Salzburg, brought on by watching *Amadeus* again. Before she could draw breath, Philip and his secretary had broken it down into flight schedules, business-class airline tickets, bookings into five-star hotels and the best seat-reservations for *The Magic Flute*.

She and Philip saw everything there was to see, in the right order, and were back home again before she could draw breath or smell an apple-strudel. And then Philip saying, "But what else did you *want*?" How could she ever explain she just wanted to get *lost*?

Anyway, she thought wryly to herself, I'm lost enough now. As the mist closed over the windmill behind, through the mist far ahead she heard the sound of gently breaking waves. They must have walked a long way in the mist, moving from crab-claw to lion's-tail seaweed to shattered fishbox marked "Smith, Lowestoft." As they walked back, they left the sea, and returned to the edge of the salt-marshes, to make sure of finding the path back to the mill.

But there were several paths, and they all looked horribly alike in the mist. And in the end they must have chosen one too far east, because the windmill was slow making its appearance, and when it did it wasn't a windmill but a low old house that hadn't been there before.

The house was very Norfolk; flint and dull red brick, except where storms had nibbled the corners, leaving patches of raw bright orange. Gable on the right, two dormer-windows in the roof on the left; all covered with massive red pantiles that made the roof sag comfortably. The hedge had grown into a fat bulging jungle that had knocked planks out of the fence in front of it.

"We can ask the way back to the mill," said Rose.

"Mu-um!" said Timothy in a voice of despair, pointing at a small damp black notice that said

TO LET OR FOR SALE APPLY BEACH HOUSE

The lettering was new, untidy but decisive. No indication of which direction Beach House lay. Obviously aimed at locals; not yuppies in need of a country retreat, like all that stuff within an hour's drive of Norwich Station. Its total unsuitability for yuppies enchanted Rose; as Jane said, "What a funny place to live. You'd never get a car up here."

Rose looked around. Maybe you could force a Land-Rover through, given half a day . . . No TVaerial on the chimney. Not an upright pole in sight, that might have carried a telephone wire or a power cable . . .

"Let's have a nosy," said Timothy.

The mother in Rose found the idea appalling. She was the least pushy of creatures. But her children looked at her, called to the child in her, as they knew they could. And the mist made it into a secret adventure.

She pushed the gate tentatively. It was dug into the ground, hanging on half a hinge. She carefully lifted it and they walked up the old brick path that meandered between clumps of invading vegetation. Long, dead plants grew up between the bricks that were visible.

"Just like Sleeping Beauty's castle," said Jane, mocking Rose's old-fashioned stories.

"Sleeping Beauty's got big feet," said Timothy, pointing to a huge pair of black rubbers sheltering under the porch.

Rose eyed the rubbers nervously. They were smeared with clay; someone had got muddy fingers taking them off, and wiped those fingers clean across the black rubber near the top. The heels were well-worn on the outsides, which should make the owner an optimist; but an optimist without the money to buy a new pair. Big feet indeed; and big feet made a big man. A big old man suddenly appearing and telling her off for trespassing, as if she were a child . . .

"I think we'd better go . . . "

"No, no," said Timothy, cunningly vanishing round the corner of the house and out of her power.

She had to follow him, to get a grip on things. But he'd found something else. Vast thin plants towering above the general weeds, with bunches of yellow flowers at the top.

"Cabbages run *wild*," he said.

"Mind they don't bite you," said Jane.

But now Rose could see, under the burgeoning weeds, gooseberry and blackcurrant bushes, the outline of a whole wrecked kitchen garden. And another brick building at the bottom of that garden.

"A little house," said Jane. "This one's mine."

"S'not," said Timothy on principle. They ran to it side by side, elbowing each other all the way. Wrestled to open one of the two doors. The building was a single-storey job, not much bigger than a hut. But it had the same sagging pantiles, and even a little brick chimney.

The first door nearly came off its hinges, as Rose got there. Over the children's heads, inside, she could see whitewashed walls, and loose flakes of whitewash spinning on the end of cobwebs. And a broad unpainted box stretching from wall to wall, with an oval hole in the middle of it.

"What *is* it?" asked Timothy. "There's a big bucket under the hole. Doesn't half niff."

"It's the bathroom," said Rose, feeling for once more knowing than her children.

"Bathroom?" said Jane, shocked. "You mean even in the middle of the night?"

"There's probably a new proper one, inside the house," said Timothy in his lordly way.

"I doubt it," said Rose smugly. Not a chance of main drainage out here, and there was no sign of

7

a septic tank. But she noticed, on the back of the outhouse door, a large rusty nail; and on the nail, large roughly-torn pieces of newspaper.

"Is that to read?" asked Jane.

"To wipe your bottom on," said Rose a trifle savagely. Spoilt little brats. That'd show them. Though, to be truthful, she'd never used newspaper in her life . . .

But far from being put off, the children were utterly fascinated. Timothy took the bundle of newspaper off the nail. It was very brown, and began to crumble between his fingers.

"This outhouse was last used on the fourth of June, 1981. *Daily Mail*. MCC weren't doing very well."

"Bighead," said Jane. "What's next door?"

"Probably the wash-house," said Rose, as she was rocked by the scramble to get past her.

It was the wash-house. With a huge iron boiler set in brick, over a tiny grate filled with white ashes.

"They boiled all their clothes in here," said Rose, lifting the lid and peering down into the boiler.

"Yuk," said the children together, holding their noses. "That's not clothes."

The boiler was full of black liquid, giving off a very putrid smell.

"That's not clothes," said Timothy. "That's *supper*!"

"Probably hasn't been used for a hundred years," said Rose with an attempt at lightness over a horrible desire to retch, as she slammed back the lid.

8

"No, Mum, no," said Timothy, bending to the grate with the pile of white ash. He extracted another triangle of brown newspaper, charred at the edges. "June the first, 1981."

For some reason, that threw Rose pretty badly. "C'mon, let's go. It's nearly lunchtime. And we've got to find the car yet."

"Aw, Mum, no!" they chorused. Timothy added, "This is the best thing we've done this holiday!"

"Better than that rotten crazy-golf at Cromer!"

"Better than *Indiana Jones*!"

"Even better than *East-Enders*!" From Jane, that was praise indeed.

For the rest of her life, Rose was to blame herself. But at the time, it was two against one. And if they chose, they could make her life heaven or hell. In her rebellion against Philip, she needed allies.

They peered through the dusty kitchen window, shading their eyes with their hands.

"No faucets," said Timothy. "Just a sort of village-pump thing. D'you think you have to pump the water up?"

" 'Spect so," said Jane. "Somebody's left the washing-up!"

Dimly, on the big kitchen table, Rose could see a mug; and a plate, with the knife and fork and some furry things still on it.

"I wonder . . . " said Timothy. And the next second he was trying the kitchen door, with its two long panes of pebbled glass, and blistered maroon paint. To Rose's horror, it swung open with a screech and Timothy vanished inside.

"Tim, no!"

But he was in the kitchen already, grimacing at her through the dusty window, putting his thumbs in his ears and wiggling his fingers. She dashed in after him, to restore order, with Jane hard on her heels.

He pointed triumphantly to a dog-eared calendar from a Norwich seed-firm that hung by the sink, and said in deep booming sinister tones, "June the eight, 1981."

Rose looked; every date til then had been crossed out, with a blue Biro cross.

"And," added Timothy, "he had bacon and egg for breakfast, and didn't finish it."

One look at the furry things on the plate nearly finished Rose.

But the next second she heard his feet thundering up the stairs.

By the time she finally got them back outside and on to the path, it was past two o'clock. And the mist was still down, and they were no nearer the car. Rose had the mildly desperate conviction that the day was going totally out of control. She had meant to take them round Holkham Hall. Or out to Blakeney Point to watch the birds.

But instead they had looked under made-up beds and found blue-flowered chamber-pots.

"Potties for grannies!"

They had got into everything, except the old

locked cupboard in the wall of the sitting-room, by the fireplace.

Timothy had opened the cases of all the old clocks, and got them ticking, if only for a minute. They had found a rusty corkscrew and a rusty can-opener with a bull's-head on it, and wanted to know how they worked. She had never known them so fascinated, so absorbed, so *gentle* . . . education, she thought, practical history. They wouldn't let them use can-openers at Holkham Hall . . .

And she herself had seldom felt so delighted, so *safe*.

"It's like Goldilocks and the Three Bears," she murmured to herself; but not softly enough.

"Oh, for God's sake, Mummy, cut the Goldilocks crap," said Jane.

"Don't use that word," said Rose. But gently. For she was totally in love with the sloping ceilings of the bedrooms, the old wallpaper with sprigs of flowers; with the old range in the kitchen, sorely in need of steel wool on the bright parts, and cleanser on the black. It was just like her own granny's. So *real*. So unlike plastic Ionic columns and computers and car phones and plane reservations for Salzburg.

Now, as she carefully closed the gate, the sun broke through the mist, for the first time that day. The low-roofed cottage seemed to *smile* at her, its reds terribly old and red and its greens so luscious-fresh she felt like eating them.

And at that very moment, Timothy said, "Hey, Mum, can we *stay* there? Live there for a bit?

We're only pissing about on this holiday. We're not going anywhere, *really*."

It cut her to the quick; half-destroyed her will, that they should guess so much. Why do we pretend our children don't notice things, she asked herself, hopelessly. Why do we comfort ourselves by pretending they're stupid?

"Don't be silly," she said feebly. "No hot water. No proper john. Nowhere within miles to park the car . . ."

"Wouldn't be any harder than *camping*," said Timothy, in his wheedling voice. That made her feel guilty, too. For years the kids had asked to go camping. But Philip said he liked comfort on his vacation, and needed to know what sort of people he was going to meet . . .

"No electricity . . . "

"Aw, c'mon, Mum! You're worse than Dad."

Timothy could not have said a deadlier thing. She looked at their two expectant cherubic hopeful faces. If they didn't get their own way, the rest of this vacation would be a *desert*. There were a million ways they could stick pins in her.

And they were such fun, when they chose to be good. Such good company.

"How would we get the cases from the car?"

"I'll do it," said Jane. "On my own." Her face was set; she really meant it.

"And what about the john in the middle of the night?"

"We could use the potties for grannies . . . "

"I'll take her down the garden," said Timothy

hastily, before Jane wrecked the scheme. "I've got my torch."

Then they both chorused, "Oh, c'mon, Mum!"

Why not? said a voice inside her. The house, for all its years of standing empty, was as dry as a bone. There was dust and rust, but nothing *dangerous*. This was England . . . And if the kids got fed up in a couple of days, it would be their own fault. And it wouldn't cost all that much . . .

She took a deep breath and said, "We'll go and see."

"Aw, Mum!" They hugged her with shining faces, as they had not done for years.

Two

Quarter of a mile up the path, they came to the village of Wallney. Not much of a village; four big farmhouses, a couple of rows of flint-and-brick cottages, pub, sub-post office and an old-fashioned red phone-box. But enough to half-restore Rose's sanity. The owner of the house wouldn't want to let it just for a week, or even a fortnight. This was no holiday cottage. The thought brought relief.

But there was the Beach House, one of the four farmhouses. Well kept, but not a working farm. Weeds grew in front of the barn doors. Rose walked up the well-kept front garden, and knocked on the door of the little glass porch. Too late, she realised the front door was never used. The porch was full of potted plants, several big ones right in front of the door itself.

An inner door opened, and a grey-haired woman in spectacles appeared. Respectable-dowdy, with sharp blue eyes and a very stubborn mouth. She gestured angrily, indicating some other entrance that should be used. It put poor Rose one-down from the start. She blundered for a long time round the barns and farmyard, trying to find a way through, until finally the woman opened a door in a six-foot wall, and looked at her as if she was an idiot.

"We've come," faltered Rose, "about renting the house. Only for a week or a fortnight . . . " She was almost ready to take to her heels and run. Only the small eager figures on each side of her kept her steady.

"Oh, come in," said the woman impatiently, and led the way with vigorous but erratic steps, as if she had arthritis but was trying to trample it underfoot by sheer will-power.

The kitchen they were led into was uncannily like the one they had just left, except it was shining and alive. There was a glowing coal fire, which cheered Rose up, even in the middle of July. A grandfather clock ticked soothingly. There was a bundle of knitting in a chair, and a tray laid for tea, with a glass sugar-basin. Various chairs were occupied by various teddy-bears, one wearing full-size spectacles.

And straightaway, Rose was under a spell. This indeed was her granny's kitchen come again. She felt very small, but very safe.

"Sit down, sit down," said the woman impatiently.

They sat, careful not to inconvenience the teddy-bears.

"We're interested in the house up the path, Mrs. . . . . "

"Miss," said the woman decisively, as if that disposed of marriage for good and all. "Miss Yaxley. Were you thinking of renting or buying? Renting is thirty pounds a week; buying is fifteen thousand freehold, including the furniture thrown in."

Rose gasped at such bluntness. And such cheapness. Why, she had more than fifteen thousand pounds of her own money. She had a sudden wild vision of herself sitting in the cottage, writing to invite Philip up for the weekend. On to her own patch. Where he would be a little diffident, and do as he was told. The prospect was *alarmingly* attractive. In order to head her imaginary letter to Philip correctly, she said, "What's the house called?"

"Beach Cottage. Belonged to my brother. Just inherited it under his will. *I've* got no use for it. Takes me all my time to keep this place going, at my time of life. Much too much for me. Much too much."

"We thought we'd like to try it for a week . . . " faltered Rose. "To see if the children like it. Then perhaps . . . "

She was sure this woman would sweep away her nonsense with a flood of biting common sense. But Miss Yaxley seemed to be very much of two minds. She turned aside, and rubbed at a tiny spot on the chrome teapot, as if it was annoying her intensely.

"It's no place for children," she said in a low voice. "My brother was an old man . . . "

"I think it's *brill*," said Timothy, turning on his most charming smile like a searchlight. He had a

16

swift eye for adult indecision. But Rose thought for once Timothy had overreached himself. Miss Yaxley gave him a grim look, as if to say children should be seen but not heard. She seemed to come to a decision and Rose was sure the answer would be no.

So she was all the more amazed when Miss Yaxley said, "Very well. I don't suppose a week can do any harm." She was still vigorously rubbing away at the spot on the teapot, which showed no sign of moving. Then she said, rather grudgingly but also rather guiltily, "I'll only charge twenty pounds for the first week. You'll have to clean the place up. Men live in *such* a muddle. They're *hopeless*. But I'd like the rent in advance. Weekly in advance."

There was more thissing and thatting, but in the end Miss Yaxley drove them back to the windmill herself in her battered Morris Minor with the dry bird-droppings turning into rust-stains on the bonnet. Rose thought that, having made her mind up, Miss Yaxley was not only keen to get them into the cottage, but also curiously keen to get rid of them.

They were done and settled in by nine. The children had truly amazed her. They'd worked like little Trojans. Rose was astonished that children could work so hard. Still, the whole thing *had* been their idea.

Timothy, who was practical like Philip, had discovered a drum of paraffin in a lean-to, filled the oil-lamps and got them going. He used more paraffin, in a careful calculating way that brought her out in a cold sweat, to get the fire in the kitchen range going. He had also got the water-pump over the sink to work. At first it had only made disgusting wheezing sounds, but Tim had poured water down it from a butt in the garden, calling it "priming the pump" very professionally. At first it had pumped evil rusty red stuff, but now it ran clear, though Rose had visions of outbreaks of cholera and typhoid, and hurried dashes to the hospital in Norwich, and how would you ever get an ambulance up that path but if you boiled all the water . . . Now he was winding up all the clocks and really getting them ticking.

And Jane had sweated up the path many times with the luggage and then gone with a huge list of groceries to the sub-post office, and staggered back again, still without complaint, and even thought to buy all available hot-water bottles. And boiled huge black kettles, and shoved all the hot-water bottles into the beds, which did seem quite clean, thank God, only awfully dusty and sneeze-making. Now she used the black kettle again to make tea, and settled down to drink hers.

"We're a nine-days' wonder in the village," she announced. "Everybody staring at me and yak, yak, yak behind their hands. The woman in the shop asked me how long we were staying, and when I said only a week to start with she said, 'Just as well, my booty, just as well.' What on earth do you think she meant by that?"

"Cholera," said Rose, in a mock-hollow voice. "Typhoid, dysentery. Double pneumonia from damp beds." She was hovering uncertainly between hilarity and hysteria.

They stared at her, amazed. Then Jane said, "Mummy made a joke."

And Timothy said, "You're quite good fun, really, Mum."

And Rose could've *wept*.

She walked up to the phone-box through the dusk. Timidly cancelled their reservation at the hotel that had been expecting them since six o'clock. Feeling very guilty, though the girl on the desk couldn't have cared less. These were hotels that Philip's secretary had booked for them, because they belonged to a branch of Philip's firm, and he got a good discount. They were comfortable but all the same inside, and boring, with fat salespeople filling the TV lounge after dinner, snoozing over quiz shows. Whereas she was *mistress* of Beach Cottage . . .

Then she rang Philip, her head whirling with excuses and defences. And got the anwering-machine. When his clear commanding voice said, "Please speak after the tone," she gabbled the address of the cottage, said, "Explain later," and fled.

The mist was returning over the salt-marshes as she walked back. Not dense, but ghosting everything, as Rose put it to herself. Making slightly and delightfully menacing shapes that turned out to be only a stunted tree, or a can of farm chemicals left on a gatepost. She felt absurdly young for thirty-eight, in a way that amazed her; she felt like kicking up her heels in spite of her tiredness. The distant glow from the windows of Beach Cottage was very welcoming, and the smoke from the chimney. This is how I felt when I was eighteen, she thought in delight. And one of a goodly company. Oh, Philip, Philip, what have you been *doing* to me?

Her children went on amazing her, through an evening of gentle lamplight and firelight. The way Jane said with authority, "I'll make the supper-drinks now." And later, shyly, "I've brought my new ghost-book. Will you read it to us, Mum? You read so well!"

Fancy her remembering, after all these years.

After the story, there was a good satisfied silence. Then Timothy said, airily.

"This place is quite *ghosty*."

"How . . . what?"

Timothy laughed at having flurried her. "S'all right, Mum. I only said *quite* ghosty. Just a little mystery, really."

"What, for heaven's sake?"

"Well, this was old Mr. Yaxley's house, right? His rubbers by the door, his dirty dishes still on the table, right? And Miss Yaxley's just inherited it, right?"

"Right!"

"So why is everything seven years out of date? As if nothing's been *touched* in here for seven years?"

It shook her. Because she couldn't think of any sensible explanation. "Oh, something legal, I expect. Legal and *boring*," she said at last.

Timothy laughed, and Jane laughed with him. "Poor old Mum," said Jane. "We won't let it get you, Mummy! Promise!"

"Yeah, promise," said Timothy, going back to reading his book on the hearthrug by the light of the fire, swinging his legs in pure contentment.

She consoled herself that they were both romantics, at least. Much more like her than Philip.

"There's a man at the back door," said Jane. "He says he's come to *do* for us."

Rose finished brushing her hair and slipped a big sweater on, over her jeans. Jane had brought her a cup of tea in bed and she'd taken it as an excuse to lie in, and listen to the sounds of the kitchen pump being cranked, the range being cleaned out, and a brisk row about how dangerous paraffin was unless you really knew what you were doing. The young master and the young mistress of the haunted castle were obviously hard at it, and she felt the urge to enjoy their efforts, while they lasted.

"What does he mean — do for us?"

"Dunno," said Jane. "I asked, and he just dropped his eyes and shuffled. I asked him in as well, but he wouldn't come."

"What does he look like?"

"He's got muddy rubbers and hairy arms and he smells a bit, but not too bad. I think he looks like a dog, but quite a *nice* dog. He says he's called Nathan Gotobed. Isn't that a *scream*?"

"Shhh," said Rose. When Jane got enthusiastic, her voice carried.

But she had to admit, when she'd flustered her way down the narrow steep dark stairs, that Mr. Gotobed did look exactly like a dog. A blunt-faced jowly sort of dog, with streaks of silver in his black hair, a farmer's three-day growth of whiskers on his face, and his spectacles mended with black adhesive tape.

The sort of dog her children had always played with on the beach, and longed for at home, and never been allowed. She sighed. She had a feeling that if the kids had their way, she was going to hear a lot of the life and times of Nathan Gotobed. They sort of collected people who drove Philip mad.

"Morning, missus," said Nathan Gotobed, touching his cap, his eyes everywhere but on her. "I've come to see to the um, you know."

He jerked his huge stubby-fingered hand towards the brick hut at the bottom of the garden. "Always saw to it in old Sepp Yaxley's day. Twice a week, though three times is better. That keep it nice and sweet."

"Yes, by all means," said Rose, her hand flying to her throat as if to choke herself lest she be tempted to mention the apparently unmentionable. "Three times a week will do nicely. Do you want paying for the erm . . . " Words failed her.

"That's up to you. You can pay at the end of the week," said Mr. Gotobed, shuffling. "When you're satisfied it's nice and sweet. And where do you want it *put*?"

"Er . . . where do you suggest?" The Green part of Rose's mind wrestled with the ecological implications.

"Sepp always liked it dug into his potato patch. Gave him some luvly good taters. But you ain't got a tater-patch no more." He surveyed the wreck of the kitchen garden with deep sorrow.

"I think you'd better just take it Away," said Rose. "Yes, Away."

"Right. Away," said Mr. Gotobed. "There's plenty as'll be glad of it, mixed with a few ashes. So ashes'll be all right then?"

"Yes, ashes will be fine," said Rose. What else was there to say?

"Just give the ashes a good stir with a stick, now and again. Keeps it sweet."

He paused, as if to consider when to See to Things. "Best done After Dark," he added. "What the eye don't see, the heart don't grieve."

"Quite," said Rose.

"Anything else you want seeing to? I only do Outsides, yer know," he added, very hastily.

Rose surveyed her Outsides — the tangled green jungle. She had the awful feeling that Philip would come roaring down to sort her out, within a week. And she would definitely be one-down if Philip saw her Outsides in this state. It seemed slightly mad to spend money on the garden when you might only stay a week, but, well, it was all slightly mad anyway.

"Could you weed the gardens? But leave any nice plants. There seem to have been some roses . . ."

"Aye. Sepp was a great man for his roses, in his day . . ."

Another profound sigh, which gave her the courage to say, "How long has Sepp . . . Mr. Yaxley . . . been . . ."

"Gone? Seven year, this June." Yet another deep sigh.

"His death must have been a great shock to you," said Rose, all sympathy.

"Dead? Who said Dead? Sepp's been gone this seven year. But I didn't say Dead."

And before she could ask more, he was lumbering down towards the brick shed that was the greater part of the Outsides. Where she did not feel inclined to follow.

She turned to see her children, apparently seriously ill with some disease that caused shining, almost tearful, eyes, bright red faces and lips pressed so close together that not even a knife could have separated them.

"Sepp's been Gone for seven years this June," said Timothy. "I didn't say Dead, I said Gone." It was a perfect imitation of Mr. Gotobed, except his voice was hollower, deeper, scarier.

"When are you having your Outsides seen to, Mummy?" Jane's impersonation was, if anything, even better.

Then they flew past her, straight to Mr. Gotobed, with the avidity of vultures coming in on a newly found kill.

She spent the morning doing housework; which she normally *loathed*. But it had to be spotless before Philip descended; Philip wouldn't have listened to Darwin, Marx or Einstein if he had found the smallest speck of dust in their studies.

Besides, this wasn't so much housework as archaeology; or playing the detective at least. She couldn't do a thing without getting to know Sepp Yaxley. His suits still hung in her wardrobe. She held one against herself. He had been a big man; six foot two at least. And an old-fashioned man indeed, given to lace-up shiny black boots, braces, suspenders and shirts with detachable collars and collar-studs. His fretwork pipe-rack made him a smoker, and the large collection of charred pipes a heavy smoker of many years' standing. And the vase of folded newspaper spills in the hearth made him a frugal man, not a waster of matches. She unfolded the spills, and found, with a slight shiver, the date June the second, 1981 . . .

In one thing, Miss Yaxley had certainly been wrong. Sepp had not been an untidy hopeless sort of man. The place was very dusty, yes, but apart from the plate and mug on the kitchen table, scrupulously tidy. He'd had no sense of arranging things to their best looking advantage, like a woman. But everything was in its grim, workmanlike place.

Which was what threw her, when she found in the bedroom that had been his (the only bedroom with a used bed and striped pyjamas under the pillow) a pocket-watch, a silver hunter, hung on a bedside stand shaped like a brass windmill.

If Sepp Yaxley had *gone*, he had gone without his watch. What kind of prudent frugal man leaves, and doesn't take his silver watch? And why hadn't Miss Yaxley taken the watch for safe-keeping? There must be thieves, even around here, and a cottage empty for seven years, with an open back door . . . It didn't add up at all, especially as no thief *had* taken it.

The watch said ten to six. But, she told herself angrily, that meant nothing. A watch can run down any time. God, I'm getting as bad as the kids . . .

But she made up her mind to take the watch to Miss Yaxley at the first opportunity. It was wrong, leaving it lying around. Putting temptation in people's way. She thought her kids were honest, if any kids were today, but even with the nicest kids . . . they were nosy little magpies, who mightn't realise the value of it. Besides, it would give her the chance to ask Miss Yaxley questions. Questions *needed* asking.

Sepp's home-made bookshelves gave her even more food for thought. All good solid old hardbacks, their spines much more faded than the rest of their covers. Paperbacks hadn't existed for Sepp Yaxley. But Karl Marx was there, well thumbed. Next to the Bible. Next to bound copies of *Old Moore's Almanac* and Nostradamus. Not an ignorant farmer; more some kind of rural sage. A book by Aleister Crowley, that she put back as if it was red-hot. Next to the *Gardener's Yearbook* . . . Then she felt the need to get on. In case Philip came.

The other thing she noticed was how busy the path to the sea had become. All kinds of folk, but mainly the elderly, strolling in leisurely fashion, carrying such a strange variety of objects; shopping bags and spades, fishing tackle and a large red cabbage. At first she thought the sunshine must have

26

brought them out. But since they returned in the other direction after a very short time, still bearing the same burdens, she formed the suspicion that the burdens were merely excuses, and that they had really come to inspect her and her family. Each, as they passed, had a word with Mr. Gotobed, hard at work in the garden.

"Now then, Nathan! How are you gittin on?"

"I'm all right, Tom."

"These'll be the children, then?"

"That's right, these be the childer."

What empty lives they must lead, she thought, shaking her duster out of the window, to make us into a great show! It also piqued her that no one noticed *her*. No eye was raised, even when she shook out the duster. No hand was waved in greeting. She would have liked to have waved back, given them a smile.

Having told her the previous night what good fun she was to be with, the children spent all the morning with Mr. Gotobed.

"Mr. Gotobed brought a great barrow-load of ashes," said Jane over lunch.

"Aye, she be right sweet now, she be!" said Timothy.

They both giggled.

"But he wouldn't go in that wash-house next door," said Timothy. "We tried to show him that yuck stuff in the boiler, but he wouldn't go near it. He was *scared* to go in. He was sweating. He told us we must never go in there, little master and missus!"

"Don't be silly!" said Rose uncomfortably.

"All right. You try him. Try offering him five pounds to empty that stuff from the boiler!"

"You mustn't pester him, or make fun of him. It's cruel!" said Rose. "Besides, what if he didn't come back? We'd be in a right mess then, wouldn't we? D'you want to walk up to Miss Yaxley's every time you want the toilet?"

That made them thoughtful; for a moment. Then Timothy said, "He's dead scared of cats, too!"

"How'd'you know that?" Rose almost snapped. After a hard morning's housework, it was too much that they were trying to scare her. She felt mildly betrayed.

"A cat came. It sat on the wall. He threw clods of earth at it. Said that cats were nasty dirty creatures that laid on newborn babes and stole their breath away. Said folks would never prosper, that kept a cat."

"Rubbish," said Rose. Then "What sort of cat was it?" Rose, all of them, were very fond of cats.

"Just an old black-and-white thing. It's all right, he didn't hit it. It dodged. We never saw it again."

Three

After lunch, Rose decided to tackle the sitting-room. It wasn't an attractive room like the kitchen. It was north-facing, full of stiff cold Victorian furniture with the blue bloom of damp on it. A room, she thought, only fit for the minister to sit in, or funerals. But Philip would want to go in there . . .

She had just started with the ancient wooden carpet-sweeper when Jane came in, saying Mr. Gotobed wanted permission to lay the hedge. Rose looked out of the window at the jungly mass of hawthorn, and said he could, and the best of British luck. As she carried on with the squeaking carpet-sweeper, she heard the thuds of heavy hacking start outside. It sounded like a massacre, and for some reason she shuddered. Maybe it was just the cold and damp in the sitting-room . . . He was certainly putting his back into it.

As she was herself. A thick cold cloud of dust

arose, seeping nastily into her throat, half-blinding her. Seven years' dust . . .

It was while she was pushing furniture around that she found the book under the big armchair by the fireplace. It was quite unlike Sepp Yaxley's other books. An old thin book bound in dull grey wrinkled leather that looked, she thought absurdly, a bit like dirty human skin. It seemed to have been sewn together by hand, with thin black twine. She opened it reluctantly. The pages were dirty and yellow, but firm and uncrumbling. They were covered with tiny hooked handwriting, not decipherable in this dim light. She had far too much to do . . . She left it on the arm of the chair, meaning to put it in the bookcase later.

Then Timothy dashed in, to say come and see how incredibly clever Mr. Gotobed was being. He was not only cutting down the hedge, he was weaving it into a kind of basket-work, half-cutting branches and twisting them over. Timothy's eager look was, as ever, irresistible. Besides, she was sick of the cold and dust. Wiping her hands on her backside, she strolled out into the warm balmy afternoon air.

The first stretch of hedge had been reduced to a narrow five-foot-high barrier, as ingeniously woven as Tim had said. It made the garden look much bigger. Mr. Gotobed stood humbly panting and touching his cap, awaiting her approval and looking more like a dog than ever. It made her feel suddenly like the lady of the manor.

"Lovely," she said. The wrinkled folds of his face split into a boyish grin, and she thought with a sudden tiny fear and sorrow that there was a hopeful schoolboy trapped, even inside the old leathery reptilian folds of Mr. Gotobed's skin.

"I'll ha' it all laid by tonight." he said. "That ain't the right season for the work, really. That's winter work, when theer's nought else to do. But the ol' hedge 'll come again awright. That's good to be hedgin' again. In the old days, brother an' me we could lay a hundred yards of hedge a day. But there in't no call for them now, with them there cutters on tractors."

"Doesn't it hurt your hands?"

"Not if you've got the right tackle." He held up his hands. His huge stubby fingers stuck out of thick black ragged leather gauntlets. One hand held a glint-edged billhook of a shape so savage it made her shudder. It might have cut down a tax-collector in the Peasants' Revolt.

"Would you like a coffee? Or a cold drink?" she said to the black weapons of massacre, afraid that her shudder might have given offence.

He said, "A cold drink would do nicely, missus." Then he caught himself and looked suddenly worried, as if he'd let himself be carried away too far by the general good humour. "If you ain't got a beer," he added cautiously.

"I haven't got beer. We've got Coke?" It seemed absurd to be offering someone out of the Peasants' Revolt a Coke. But he beamed at her now.

"Coke 'll do fine, missus. I like a nice Coke."

"Come in, then, come in!" She led the way into the kitchen. "Straight from the can, or would you like a glass?"

31

No answer. She turned, and found he was no-where to be seen. Baffled, she went outside again. He was sitting in the boiling sun, on an old bench by the kitchen door.

"*Do* come in! It's cool in the kitchen! You could do with cooling off!"

"No, missus, I'll stop here. Sepp Yaxley allus let me sit here, when I was restin'!" Behind his mended glasses, his face was stubborn, defiant, unknowable. Like a thick-skinned reptile's again. But there was the slightest quaver of panic in his voice, and his hands were shaking, though that might have been just the exertion.

"Oh, suit yourself," she said, a bit put out; and got the can of Coke and gave it to him. Watched those thick stubby fingers pull at the tab, and need three tries to do it. His hands really were trembling.

Oh, really, it was just age and exertion.

There seemed nothing else to say, so she went back to her dusting.

She left the mantelpiece till last. It was crammed with stuff. An American clock, that Tim had failed to get going. Several big bits of Staffordshire pottery, with whole arms and legs missing. Bundles of papers behind every one. An avalanche waiting to fall.

She started cautiously at the left-hand end. A miniature brass milk-churn with a lid. But, careful as she was, she nearly dropped it. It weighed a ton. The thin wire handle cut into her fingers. Must be full of lead . . .

She put it on the table and took the lid off and

peered inside. It seemed full of pound coins; but oddly shiny new pound coins. Surely pound coins had come in less than seven years ago? She tipped them out. No, they weren't pound coins. Too thin. A Queen's head on them, but the wrong Queen . . . Victoria. She turned one of them over.

Dear God, they were sovereigns!

Sixty-four *gold* sovereigns. By the time she had finished counting them, her own hands were trembling. She had nearly ten thousand pounds under her fingers.

Astonishment turned into sudden fury. Leaving such money in a house let to visitors! Where there were children . . . it was *criminal*. Accusations of theft could start at any moment! A silver watch was bad enough, but *this* . . . !

She was going up to give Miss Yaxley a piece of her mind. She shovelled the sovereigns viciously back into the churn, and was just marching to the door when another thought struck her.

Was there anything else?

She searched the rest of the mantelpiece with the grim thoroughness of a police inspector. It was as well she did. A teapot with a chipped spout. Full of greasy five-pound notes. Over a thousand pounds!

She shoved the lot into a tote bag, washed her hands, put on makeup and set out. As she went out the front gate, Mr. Gotobed was giving Jane a lesson in hedge-laying.

"Hack *away* from yourself or you'll have your fut off in a minute. Sideways, away from ye'. Like this!"

33

"Won't be long — just nipping up to the village," she called. In a tone of cold fury that made Tim peer over the hedge at her, his face wrinkled up in bafflement.

"Oh, you've brought Sepp's watch," said Miss Yaxley, picking it up with a satisfied tightening of her lips. "It was his father's watch before him."

Rose banged the milk-churn down on the table.

"An' his sovereigns! He always liked sovereigns, did Sepp. Collected them when he was a boy. Said *they'd* never rot!"

Rose banged down the teapot, with a force that threatened further damage to it.

"An' his petty cash!" said Miss Yaxley.

"A thousand pounds," said Rose, ominously.

"He was never short of a dollar, Sepp." Miss Yaxley calmly shoved the money back into the teapot, and put the lid back on. She was showing no emotion at all. Rose felt so weird she almost let Miss Yaxley get away with it, as she matter-of-factly stowed the stuff on her own mantelpiece.

"I think I'm owed *some* explanation. My children might have . . . !"

"I saw you had an honest face," said Miss Yaxley. "Or I wouldn't have let the cottage. I knew you'd be up . . . "

"That's not the point. They've been lying there *seven years*. With the back door open. Anyone could've taken them, young tearaways . . . "

"We don't have young tearaways round here."

"You *amaze* me."

34

"Anyway, nobody round here would touch Sepp's things."

"Why NOT?"

"It was wi' the lawyers. In the hands o' the lawyers. Sepp wasn't legally dead, til this June. We couldn't touch none of his stuff. Would be agin the law."

"Then why didn't the lawyers take charge of the valuables?"

"Pro'bly they didn't know he had any."

"Why didn't you tell them?"

"They never asked me."

Rose felt she was being led round in circles. She grasped for any solid fact in this madness. Desperation made her ruder than she ever usually was.

"Would you mind telling me what exactly happened to your brother, Miss Yaxley?"

"He just . . . went. Went out one morning an' never came back. I don't even know what morning it was. He always came up for his tea Fridays, and he didn't come that week. Second week he didn't come, I told the poliss."

"Didn't the police search?"

Miss Yaxley shrugged, head down. "They did, but . . . Sepp went out on the marshes a lot. Caught things. Tide can be treach'rous. Seven years you have to wait, before you can declare un dead. If there's no body."

"But surely you could clear up his house?"

"Got enough to do here. Sepp an' me weren't that close."

It was like beating your head against a brick wall,

35

Rose thought. It was like being in the mist again. It was as if Miss Yaxley were speaking to her from a different land, where different rules applied. Where city people, police, even the law itself were a stupid uncomprehending nuisance. An older time . . .

"I find all this totally incredible," she said.

"Ain't none of your business, is it? You come down here in your big motor with your two pretty children . . . what are we to you? You can go or stay as you like. Though what you find to do round here . . . "

There was faint *disgust* in Miss Yaxley's voice. The disgust of the rural for the urban. The disgust of the real for the unreal. The same disgust she herself felt for car phones and computers and yuppies. She felt the ground move beneath her, felt herself being pushed out of . . .

"I'm sorry," she said abruptly. "It is none of my business."

"No bones broken, moi dear." Miss Yaxley too seemed to regret the clash, and want to make amends. "Thank you for bringing Sepp's things. The money will come in nicely."

"Be careful when you take it to the bank. I think it's illegal now, to hold so many sovereigns; if you're not a bullion-dealer."

"Not my crime, moi dear. An' Sepp's dead, isn't he? Besides, folks don't hold with banks much, round here."

"Can we . . . stay on? At the cottage?"

"Stay as long as you like, moi dear. If that's what you want."

36

"We've got a man seeing to us. Nathan Go-tobed."

"Aye," said Miss Yaxley. "So I've heard. He did for Sepp." She said it with a hint of . . . Rose could not fathom what she'd said it with a hint of.

When she got home, Timothy and Jane were still tucking in bits of the newly laid fence.

But Nathan Gotobed and his terrible billhook were gone. And the hedge was only half-laid.

"A man came for him," said Timothy. "They had an argument."

"What about?"

"We couldn't hear. Did you find out anything else about Mr. Yaxley?"

She gave him a startled look. "Why did you ask that?"

"Oh," he said with an airy shrug. "We just thought you might have heard some gossip in the shop." Jane shrugged inscrutably as well.

Rose had that awful feeling that everybody was hiding something from her. But she just said shortly, "They think he got drowned on the marshes."

"Oh," said Timothy. "That's odd."

"*What's* odd, for heaven's sake?"

"I thought he'd wear his rubbers to go on the marshes. And his rubbers are still here."

Rose couldn't settle to dusting again. She felt restless, which disturbed her, because she wasn't normally a restless person. Perhaps it was just the contrast between the warm sunny day outside, and the dimness of the house. She felt things were going on outside and she was missing them. She rationalised it into a trip to the shop. Jane made strenuous offers to go for her, but Rose said tartly, "*My* turn for a nosy!"

As she re-entered the village, her white Volkswagen Golf gave her an appealing look. It seemed terribly stranded and lonely stuck on the grass shoulder where the road ended and the path began. She felt a vague unease at the car being so far from the house, instead of parked in the drive as usual. She always thought it ironical, afterwards, that the first unease she felt was about the car . . .

She checked the doors and trunk. Locked. But, inscribed on the dusty hood by a small finger, she found the legend

THIS CAR IS DIRTY

She smiled a little, because children were the same everywhere. Then she walked round checking the tires. And found scrawled on the trunk-lid, by a bigger finger, the single word

YUPPIE!

Somehow, because the finger had been bigger, it upset her much more. And because she couldn't have been further from being a yuppie. She got a sense of prejudice, determined ignorance, deliberate unfairness. A sense it was perhaps unfortunate she carried into the shop.

It wasn't a big shop, and there had been a pathetic attempt to turn it into a mini-market, which made it seem even smaller. Where she had hoped to find brass scales, round blocks of real cheese and enamel adverts for Fry's Milk Chocolate, she found the thin blue and white stripes of Mace, and garish star-shaped price tags in fluorescent orange. There were one or two women idly contemplating the same old brands with a total absorption that would have done credit to the Buddha himself. Her approach had obviously been observed.

The two shopkeepers stood behind their cash-register, as oddly assorted a couple as she'd ever seen. The man was tall and thin, with a balding sallow streetwise face that could never have been born in East Anglia. He had made some attempt to dress sportingly in an Arsenal sweatshirt, but there was dirt down the front of it from handling boxes. His wife was short and stout, with a very humped back under her navy print dress, and an upper lip and chin that had those straggling strands of facial hair that always made Rose want to curl up inside.

"Aha," said the man. "Tracked us down at last, I see!" He spoke loudly, for the benefit of the whole shop, with that kind of bumptious flirtatiousness and familiarity that always whines, when tackled head-on, that it means no harm, just a bit of fun, can't you take a bit of fun?

"Good afternoon," said Rose stiffly.

"From London, are we?" The man's grin was subtly offensive. Rose supposed that being the only source of groceries in the village, he could afford to offend his customers. She even began to think kindly of the impersonality of supermarkets.

She snapped, "Richmond, actually! How did you know where I came from?"

"Garage name on your car's big enough," said the man.

Was he the one whose finger had written "Yuppie"?

"Anyway," said the man, "those of us from south of the river must stick together among these local yokels."

Rose sensed the female backs behind her stiffen; the silence in the shop had become electric.

"I like country people very much," she said.

"Jack Sydenham from Battersea," he said, sticking his hand out.

"Six boxes of Swan Vestas," said Rose, nodding at the tobacco shelf behind the counter. The hairy-backed hand faltered, despaired, and fumbled for the matches.

"Big smoker, then?"

"Oil-lamps to light."

"Yes, he didn't have many mod cons, did old Sepp Yaxley. Settling in all right, though, are you?"

"Quite comfortably, thank you." Rose was startled at the haughty frostiness of her own voice.

"Saw you going up to see old Miss Yaxley. Yer bag was heavier going in than it was coming out again!"

"Just a few things Miss Yaxley wanted."

She felt the silence in the shop deepen, if that were possible.

"You haven't found his crock o' gold, have yer? Old Sepp was famous for the crock o' gold he had stashed away." The man's eyes were shining, his lips slightly parted, as if he was enjoying playing with fire.

But before Rose could say, "I think that's Miss Yaxley's business," the woman behind the counter said, "We need some more Lilt, Jack. Go and get me a case of Lilt from the back. I'll see to the lady."

It seemed an inoffensive enough remark to make, but the tone was dismissive. The light went out of Jack's eyes, and he went without a word. Did Rose hear breaths quietly let out, all round the shop? What *was* it with Sepp Yaxley?

The woman was pleasant enough, in her way, and brisk and helpful.

"Don't these other ladies want serving first?" asked Rose politely.

"Oh, they won't mind, moi dear." The woman's voice was truly Norfolk. "They're only passing the time o' day." She grabbed Rose's tote bag, where it lay on the counter, and filled it briskly and efficiently with groceries.

She also took a good look inside it. She was subtler than her husband, but she didn't bother to be all that subtle . . .

Rose left the mini-market vowing to shop in Cley in future. She went back to the car, and hovered unhappily. She wished she could take it home with her. She glanced in through the windows. There wasn't much to see. Just magazines on the back shelf. A *Good Houskeeping* of her own, an *Indy* of Timothy's, a *Jackie* of Jane's. And Jane's spare pair of headphones for her Walkman. But Rose suddenly saw the objects as prying alien eyes must have seen them. A rich bitch and her two over-privileged spoilt brats . . .

"Hallo," said a small voice at her elbow. It was a little girl, of the type given to accosting strangers with a knowing charm. The child dimpled. "You're the lady from the Cunning's house, aren't you?"

"The Cummings' house?" Rose frowned. Had there been someone called Cummings living there, before Sepp Yaxley?

"No, no," the child frowned in unconscious mimicry of her. "Not the Cummings' house — the *Cunning's* house." She gnashed her teeth over the n's in a way that was almost animal.

"You mean the Cunninghams' house?" persisted Rose. She always believed in being patient with children.

"No, no, no," said the child. "The Cunning's house."

Rose gave up. Was everyone a bit mad in this village? She walked on back down the path. The child watched her go a long time, putting her thumb in her mouth.

The child had done her best. It was a pity that Rose knew little of the older customs of East Anglia.

After supper, she walked up to Wallney again, to ring Philip. Bracing herself for the encounter. Making his voice say, inside her head, the things he would say, and practising her smooth calm answers.

"Rose, what the devil are you up to?"

42

"Having a holiday!"

"What's your phone number?"

"We haven't got a phone number!"

"Then how the devil am I supposed to get in touch with you, if something comes up?"

"Why not write? Or drive up and see us?'

"Now look, Rose! If this is another of your crazy schemes . . . "

But when she rang the number, a neatly arranged pile of silver on the shelf of the phone-booth beside her elbow, she got only the answering machine again, and all her witty replies died within her.

Coming back, a little vexed but not yet alarmed, through a slight rising mist, she saw a cat sitting on the wall. A tabby cat. Not the one Mr. Gotobed had thrown clods at, then . . .

She went out of her way to woo it, as a kind of defiance of all the invincible ignorance that Wallney stood for. She did what the best cat-books told you to do with a stray cat, to avoid alarming it. She did not look at it directly. She yawned and stretched her arms gently above her head; anyone watching her would have thought her a lunatic.

But the only one watching her was the cat. And on the cat, all her efforts were wasted. It made no attempt to flee, but continued sitting solidly on the wall. Its ears neither went down in alarm, nor pricked in curiosity. It needed no assurance that she was harmless. From long instinct, it knew she was harmless. It let her get within a foot; it let her put out her hand to stroke, with apparent indifference.

She was shocked at how solid it was; at the hardness of the muscles under its dark tiger-stripes. She was shocked at the intricate mangling of its torn ears, at the brutal massiveness of its wedge-shaped head.

It did none of the things that cats are supposed to do. It did not rub its cheeks against her hand, or offer its chin; it did not knead its paws on the wall-top, or arch its back. It certainly did not purr. Its eyes studied the flight of birds across some distant field.

In the end, it made her feel irrelevant and powerless. It offered her no threat of violence, but she came to think it was not a nice cat. She even grew a little nervous of its dark indifference to human kind.

She finally went on her way, much put out. Thinking it was another bit of that massive ignorance, that brutal imperviousness that was Wallney.

The cat watched her go. Watched her turn in at the gate where it knew she lived. Then, as if satisfied, it dropped down into the field behind the wall, and went about its own business.

Four

It was good to be home. There was a huge fire glowing in the kitchen range; a little too hot for comfort, but the kids' willingness was warming, too, after Wallney. They looked up from the books they were reading, and the fire shone on the pleasure in their faces at her return.

"I went up to turn down the beds," said Jane. "There's a mouse in my bedroom."

"What did you do?" said Rose in a flurry. She always felt irretrievably split about mice. You read in magazines that their urine gave children diseases, yet they were so timid, furry and defenceless. She had never had to cope with a mouse in her married life. Mice did not come where Philip was . . .

"It was sweet," said Jane. "I took it up some cheese. I thought it might be starving. I mean, what's it had to live on round here all these years? But it wouldn't come out of its hole for the cheese."

"She bunged the cheese down the hole in the end," said Timothy. "The lump got stuck. The mouse can't get out, now."

"It can *eat* its way out," said Jane.

"How would you like to have to *eat* your way out?" said Tim. "If you opened this door in the morning, and somebody had dumped a ton of liver pâté on the doorstep?"

"I expect it will survive," said Rose hurriedly, before World War III could develop. "Want to play something before bed?" She moved over to the heap of boxes; Monopoly, Othello, Trivial Pursuit; Genus II that went with them on every holiday.

"Can we play Dirty Scrabble?" asked Jane. "Only Daddy won't let us at home." Rose shuddered; they knew so many appalling words *she* had never known till she went to university. And Jane always objected to Tim's scientific Latin ones, sticking to awful Anglo-Saxon herself. They never said them out loud, it was true, but as you went on playing, the words already laid down stared at you so, and made you giggle. And it was wrong to giggle; it let down the grownup side.

"It was a fieldmouse," said Jane. "I know, cos their tails are longer."

"Tripe," said Timothy. "It was just an ordinary house-mouse. Fieldmice don't invade a house till winter . . . "

46

"How do you know, Clever Dick? It might have been a harvest mouse, the sort the Romans brought."

"Have you ever *seen* a harvest mouse, even in a *book*?"

"All right," said Rose hastily. "Dirty Scrabble it is."

It was their last happy evening.

At lunch the next day, Jane said, "Mr. Gotobed's going to build you a rockery . . . "

"A rockery? Whatever for?"

"You can't beat a nice little rockery, moi booty! With little plants a-growin' hare and there!" Uncannily Mr. Gotobed's old gravelly voice issued from her son's soft childish lips.

"But I don't *want* a rockery. And Miss Yaxley hasn't even been consulted . . . "

"Too late," said Timothy. "He's gone for a load of them stones."

"But where is he going to get *stones* round here? There *aren't* any stones. And he hasn't finished the hedge-laying yet."

"I know. That's the funny thing. He was laying the hedge quite happily, till he found what the rabbits had done."

"Rabbits?" Rose's mind began to sway again.

"Rabbits in the garden, digging burrows. We found them and showed him. They weren't very good burrows, not very deep. Three of them, all in one group. Mr. Gotobed filled them in again, and stamped the earth down hard. Said you didn't

47

want rabbits in a garden, they ate all the lettuce and cabbages."

"But we haven't got any lettuces and cabbages worth saving . . . "

"I know. We said that. But then he told us about building the rockery, and went off in a hurry."

There was a sound of grinding outside, as they finished up their rather horrible fruits of the forest low fat yogurts, from the mini-market. A grinding as of iron on stone, a rumbling, then an enormous thump. Then a second grinding and thump; then a third.

They rushed out, to see three figures departing down the path, wheeling wheelbarrows. The first two figures were of young men in washed-out jeans, but otherwise stripped to almost the level of the crack between their buttocks. They were bronzed and muscled like young Greek gods. The sort of men Rose always felt she shouldn't be looking at, as they rested on their shovels at some roadworks, and Rose was stuck in the resulting traffic-jam.

The last of the trio was the well-wrapped-up form of Mr. Gotobed. He turned, when he was a good distance away, and waved reassuringly.

Rose thought she ought to hurry after him. Unfortunately, entirely blocking the gate was a large and unstable heap of sharp-edged stone, quite unnavigable to anyone wearing Clarks sandals, as Rose was. To anyone wearing less than very large hobnailed boots . . .

The stone was a curious mixture; some good brown sandstone blocks, that looked as if they'd been filched from a historic monument; a lot of round stones about six inches in diameter, that Timothy said must have come from the fields; and lastly a lot of ugly shattered reinforced concrete, with rusty bits of reinforcement still sticking out of it.

Timothy surveyed the treacherous and unsightly heap. "Now we know how the mouse felt," he said, to nobody in particular.

By the time they had returned with three more barrowloads of stone, the argument was unwinnable. Rose just hadn't the heart to make them take it all away again. They looked so hot and sweaty! And they meant so well; their grins were so boyish and pleased with themselves. She opened her mouth to chide, but only the offer of a cold drink came out.

They all, instantly, said, "Coke please, missus." And then the two young gods were introduced as Harry and Dave, and enthusiastically shook hands with everyone having first wiped their hands on their worn-out jeans with such vigor that poor Rose expected strands of pubic hair to become visible above their faded belts at any moment.

Rose might, she supposed, have still kicked up a fuss had they intended to put the rockery somewhere quite unsuitable, like the middle of the front garden. But in the end they built it on a narrow patch by the path to the outhouse, close under the shadow of the hedge. She was so relieved at the site they had chosen that she felt almost grateful to them. They carried stone all the afternoon with great energy. Rose worried about how to pay them; but Timothy came back with the message that all they required was more Coke, and Jane went whizzing up to the shop for it. Then, quite suddenly, the gateway was clear of stone again, and they were gone, and she hadn't got to worry about their jeans falling down any more, and Mr. Gotobed was back to his hedge-laying, whistling to himself like a man with a job well done. Rose went to inspect the new rockery, tactfully, since he had made no attempt to show it to her. She had to admit they had made the best of a bad job. The pieces of concrete were towards the back, turned cunningly so that soil covered the twisting, rusted reinforcement wires. The big blocks of sandstone had been set on edge, so their corners jutted up like minute mountains. The smaller round stones had been wedged tightly between, not leaving an inch of soil exposed. The whole effect was of a decaying bit of Hitler's West Wall, in miniature. With tank-traps. Rose told herself it was the kind thought that mattered . . .

By the time he went home, Mr. Gotobed had nearly finished the hedge-laying. The only bit of hedge untouched was the bit that overshadowed the tank-traps. But in his erratic way, he had left it, in the last half-hour of work, and turned his attention again to weeding the front garden. Rose told herself to be charitable. It would be awkward to lay that bit of hedge now, swinging the billhook standing on tiny pinnacles of sandstone. Of course, he should have thought of that before he made the damned rockery! But then, she didn't think he could be all that bright . . .

The children were oddly troubled over supper. She kept on looking up from the Cornish pasties heated in the oven of the range, and peas and potatos boiled on the open fire, to see them exchanging looks, nods and shrugs. Which they stopped, as soon as they saw her watching.

She looked down at her plate, carefully slicing off a triangular corner of pasty as neatly as a surgeon, and said suddenly, "All right, what's going on?"

"You tell her."

"No, you!"

After quite a lot of this, Timothy said, "Mr. Gotobed's set snares for rabbits in the garden. They're very cunning — you can hardly see them cos he's wrapped grass round them — but I wondered what he was fiddling with so much, and after he'd gone, I looked."

"Snares?" Rose's blood was up in a second. "Do you know how snares work? Do you know how cruel they are? The rabbit's neck goes through the loop, when it's running along a path, and the rabbit struggles to get out and the noose tightens and tightens, until the rabbit slowly chokes to death. If it doesn't choke on its own blood. Where *are* these snares?"

Timothy had gone a bit white. "I'll show you, Mum. There's three . . . " He led the small and shocked procession out of doors.

The first was not far from the front gate. It was

right against the hedge, opposite a small hole in the bottom of the hawthorns, where some small creature seemed to have worn a path in the long grass.

"The rabbit comes running through there," said Rose. "And," she thrust her hand and wrist along the tiny faint path, and a noose of plaited grass closed tightly round her wrist; tightly enough to crease her pale flesh. And inside the plait of grass was the glint of plaited copper wire. And on the end of the loop of wire, a length of strong dull-brown cord. And then she heaved, and a big soily peg like a tent-peg came out of the ground with a flurry of earth. "That's how a snare works!" She added, "I'm going to throw it in the trash can."

"There isn't one, Mum," said Jane thoughtfully.

"Mr. Gotobed takes all the rubbish away," said Timothy.

"They *are* his snares," said Jane. "They look like they cost quite a lot of money . . . " Her voice was slightly shocked.

"Whose side are you on?" demanded Rose. Then she said, "I shall *speak* to him, in the morning. Go and fetch the other two snares, Tim. And make sure you don't hurt yourself . . . "

But Tim seemed to have seen something in the surrounding grass.

"Here's one of the rabbit's hairs," he said. "It's very *dark*, for a rabbit."

"You get black rabbits," said Jane. "Witches used to keep black rabbits as familiars . . . "

"What — in *East-Enders*?" asked Timothy, with mock-serious interest.

"No — in a book called *Matthew Hopkins, Witchfinder-general* — clever!"

"Oh, Matthew Hopkins — he's in *Dallas*. I forgot."

"Why do you always try to make out I'm stupid when you go on and on making stupid remarks yourself that you think are funny and nobody else does only they're too polite to say so . . . "

"It's getting cold," said Rose. "Let's get back indoors."

She was just saying it to be tactful.

So why did she shiver?

They were bedded down for the night, in the low dim bedrooms with their sloping ceilings. The exchange of insults from bedroom to bedroom had finally ceased. Jane at least had put out her oil-lamp, for her bedroom showed dark through the half-opened doors. She wondered if Tim had fallen asleep over his book with the light still on; then she heard him turn a page, the night was so silent.

She turned her own page. She wished she had a more suitable book, like *Lark Rise to Candleford* or Kilvert's diary, but all she had was one of Philip's violent thrillers, brought home from a transatlantic flight. Though it was as much about suspender-belts as guns . . . she thought sadly that after all, he *was* a Cambridge graduate, even if it was in science. What did men see in such books, where the women were as cold and hard as the tiny blue-barrelled automatics they produced from their stocking-tops?

The noise was a tearing of the night, a murder of the silence. It rose and cracked, as if the throat that made it could no longer sustain it. Inhuman, unearthly. Rose's legs gave a convulsive twitch under the bedclothes. Then the noise rose again . . .

Outside. In the dark. In the garden.

A third time it rose. And then Jane came flying into the room and hurled herself on to the bed and into Rose's arms.

"Mummy, what is it? I thought I was having a nightmare but . . . "

The noise rose a fourth time. Savage. Yet mournful, as if there were no hope, no life left in the world. Cold and dreary as death itself, Rose thought.

A movement in the doorway made Rose's skin leap all over. But it was only Timothy. He looked quite calm; almost as if he was enjoying himself. There was something long and black in his hands. His hands tensed, as he bent it in half . . .

"Tim, what have you got?"

He gave a small grin. "Only my air-pistol. The one Dad gave me last Christmas. I thought it might come in useful in outlandish parts . . . "

"Tim, for heaven's sake, what good is an *air-pistol*?"

"It's a .22. It can go through a plank of wood at fifty yards. Dad and I tried it, down Bunty's pit. It's Yugoslav — "

"Tim, you wouldn't shoot . . . "

"Bloody would," he said, taking a small shiny pellet from the box that was bulging his pyjama pocket and putting it carefully into the barrel. He closed the air-pistol with a reassuring click.

The awful cry rose again, as Tim parted the curtains and opened the small window. "Black as the hobs of hell out here," said his suddenly muffled voice.

Rose leapt out of bed. If her offspring was going to shoot something on her behalf, she really ought to be there as a witness. She pushed in alongside him, in the narrow dormer window. Peered out. There was a dim blue light to the south; the one solitary neon streetlamp in the centre of Wallney, by the sub-post office. And the moon was somewhere up there, behind clouds . . . As her eyes grew accustomed to the dimness, she began to see the line of the laid hedge.

"There it is," said Tim. "On the rockery."

There was a small black shape, on the faint paleness of the concrete lumps.

Her breath went out of her in a great whoosh. "It's only cats . . . tomcats fighting."

"I can only see one of them."

"The other one must be in the hedge."

"But there's only one making a noise. And it's not hunched up like it's going to fight. It's just *sitting*."

Another wail went up. In spite of knowing it was a cat, Rose couldn't help shuddering. "I hope it goes away soon."

"Shall I have a pot at it?" Tim raised the pistol.

"Tim, how *could* you?" This was a crueller Tim than she'd known before; she felt distress, that she didn't know her own children better.

"I don't mean to *hit* it. Or only on the end of the tail, to scare it away. I'm a dead shot, you know."

"Certainly not. If we ignore it, it will soon go away. It's time you were tucked up with your light out."

"Oh, all right. I'll have to fire the gun though. You can't unload it." The gun gave a vicious spat, and there was a sharp thud from down the garden.

"Outhouse door," said Tim. "Have a look at the hole it's made, in the morning."

"Tim, *really!*"

But with a rather sinister little giggle, he had slipped away to bed.

She went back to bed in a fluster. Really, damaging people's property . . . he needed a father's hand.

Which reminded her that she hadn't tried to phone Philip this evening. She'd just *forgotten*. What was she coming to? It was all that upset about the rockery. Everyone was being so very odd.

And that damned cat went on yowling and yowling, fit to wake the dead.

She finally managed to get to sleep by jamming a pillow over her ear. She'd only ever read about people doing that before.

She wakened feeling leaden and weary. Breakfast

was a chore to make, because the fire in the range had gone out, in spite of careful banking-up. The kids were weary too. It was a morose meal, during which Rose several times asked herself what the heck she was doing here, instead of sitting down to fresh coffee and croissants in some four-star hotel. This was supposed to be a *vacation*, for God's sake!

She went back to cleaning the sitting-room, telling the kids to ask Mr. Gotobed to come and see her as soon as he got here. She was still angry about the snares, and even more angry about the half-inch hole in the outhouse door. That gun was a terrifying thing; the pellet had gone through the outhouse seat too. Mr. Gotobed would certainly notice, and might go and tell Miss Yaxley. Philip had been totally irresponsible buying Timothy a lethal weapon like that. She was cross with nearly everybody.

And she was cross with the dimness of the sitting-room, even on a sunny morning. In a fit of reluctance to start, she idly picked up the book that she'd found under the armchair. Such *funny* writing. The way you thought you could just about read it, then found when you focused your eyes that you couldn't. It didn't seem to be in any foreign language; she knew French and German, and could recognise most European languages. It seemed more like abbreviated English. "Wth" might be "with," for instance . . .

"You wanted me, missus?" The small open window darkened, and she looked up to see Mr. Gotobed standing outside. He had a truculent look on his face; she somehow knew that he knew about the snares. Oh, God, more bother! She walked to the window, studying Mr. Gotobed's face. His eyes were slitty, and his mouth turned down.

And then his eyes dropped to the level of her navel. His mouth fell open, displaying a decaying graveyard of leaning teeth. His eyes, from being slitty, went very wide; she could quite distinctly see the whites all round them. She thought, as he looked her in the face again, that he was about to scream. He had certainly gone very pale; his unshaven whiskers stood out like dark paint. Perhaps he was going to have a stroke or a heart attack . . .

Instinctively, she reached out her free hand.

"Mr. Gotobed . . . "

He backed away from her hand as if it held a viper.

His mouth made a couple of movements and a moan came out. And then suddenly he wasn't there any more. He was running down the garden path, as fast as his old legs would carry him. He flung open the front gate so savagely that it fell off its remaining hinge. And then he was just a head bobbing away down the lane.

Two more heads appeared at the window, as she stood paralysed.

"What did you say to Mr. Gotobed?" asked Tim in an awed voice.

"I only said, 'Mr. Gotobed,' " said Rose, helplessly. "Then he ran off. He looked terrified. Why should he suddenly be terrified of *me*?"

Her children looked at her, with disconcerting seriousness.

"Your hair needs combing," said Jane. "And you're not wearing any makeup. But you never do, in the mornings."

"Bare feet in sandals," said Tim severely. "It must be your hippy image, Mum." She realised with relief that their seriousness was only mockery.

"But why? He sort of looked at my tummy, and then he moaned and ran."

"Your shirt's out and hanging down under your sweater," said Tim. "But he's a grown man! Perhaps he fancies you, Mum. Perhaps you aroused his lust to breaking point . . . "

"Be *serious*." Rose was on the verge of tears. It was the first time she had ever terrified anybody in her life.

"Were you holding that book?" said Jane sharply. "*How* were you holding it?"

She showed them.

"In front of your tummy," said Jane. "He must have been looking at that book."

"But why . . . a book?"

Jane took the book from her. "It's a very odd-looking book. You can't read the writing. Perhaps it's a book of spells . . . "

"Bollocks," said Timothy. "It's handwriting. 'Spect it's old Yaxley's secret diary. Maybe he was keeping records on everybody in the village, and blackmailing them. Maybe Mr. Gotobed thought you were going to blackmail *him*."

59

"But what . . . " The idea of Mr. Gotobed being blackmailed was ridiculous.

"Poaching rabbits?" suggested Tim. "Growing marijuana on his allotment? Getting the milkmaids preggers?"

"Oh, don't be so ridiculous."

"He's left his wheelbarrow and his tools and everything. What shall we do if he doesn't come back? Who's going to see to us?"

"I'd better go and talk to him, I suppose," said Rose wearily.

"But he's terrified of *you*," said Tim. The kids looked at each other. "He's not terrified of us. We'll go and talk to him. Take him his wheelbarrow. That'll be a good excuse." They nodded to each other, with secretive grins. They were really raring to go.

It was against Rose's better judgement. But she had lost most of her faith in her own judgement. She was badly shaken. People had always taken to her on sight. People came to her to talk about their troubles. Harmless kind Rose. And now she felt like some kind of monster . . .

"All right," she said. "And if he won't come back, ask him how much we owe him."

She went up to her bedroom. She watched them set off up the lane, chattering excitedly, off on a great expedition. Then she looked at herself in the dim, fly-spotted mirror of the dressing-table. Large brown eyes; they were her best feature. Kind eyes, even if they did have smudges under them this morning. A high clear forehead, even if it was showing a few wrinkles. A generous mouth, and

60

not quite enough chin; that was why people had always known she was harmless. Not any kind of monster . . .

The house was too quiet now. She didn't want to stay in it, with the kids gone. Didn't want to be alone with that stupid book downstairs . . .

She decided she would go and walk by the sea; it would soothe her.

Five

Halfway down the long path to the sea, she began to get the absurd idea that she was being followed. She told herself as usual not to be silly. It was just that this path was so long and straight and narrow. It felt like walking down a ruler. The narrowness and the high unkempt hedges, and the utter boringness of the fields on either side, which gave you no excuse to turn off into them . . . if you saw somebody a long way off, or a long way behind, you would be trapped into passing them eventually; there was no way of avoiding people.

But why should she *want* to avoid people? You would just smile and nod, and squeeze past, and that would be that. And usually, in the country, she *liked* meeting people. God, I'm getting neurotic, she thought. A few days away from the dominating safety of Philip and I'm getting neurotic. I don't deserve to be an independent woman. Snap out of it, girl!

But the back of her neck went on prickling, as if someone *was* following her, *was* watching. Oh, surely the prickling was just the breeze blowing little stray strands of hair against the soft skin at the back of her neck . . .

Having satisfied herself with this entirely rational and scientific explanation, she immediately turned and looked behind.

Someone *was* following her. A man, only about a hundred yards behind. She got only a brief glimpse, before she turned her head back to the front, feeling the traitorous flush of embarrassment staining her cheeks. But she had seen enough. That tall unbowed figure was no slow-plodding farmworker. It was walking with a brisk city gait. And it was wearing a trilby hat, which looked absurd with the bright banded sweatshirt. Only one man in Wallney would be fool enough to turn himself out like that for a walk. Jack Sydenham; the stupid, cocky and revolting Jack Sydenham.

But, stupid and revolting though he was, he was still a *man*. The loneliness of this spot made that the most important fact about him. A man, bigger and stronger than she was. And she was letting him herd her like a sheep, drive her further and further from the safety of her house.

With a spurt of rage, she decided to call his bluff. She would face him out. She would lean against the next gate and wait for him to pass her.

She found her gate and leaned against it. She considered pulling out a long stem of grass and chewing it, to show just how casual she felt about him. But she decided against it; it would only give him an opening for one of his stupid remarks . . . So she just waited, feeling his eyes tickling over her cheek and jaw, terrified her thin skin would blush again, and give her away. She heard the swish of grass, the slight thud of his foot upon bare soil, the crunch on the odd patch of gravel some farmer had once used to mend the path.

"Morning," said Jack Sydenham, in a falsely-hearty voice. "Nice morning for a walk!"

She turned, feigning surprise. "Oh, Mr. Sydenham! Are you taking a day off, too? Things slack at the shop?"

His knowing eyes dropped; the knowing grin was wiped off his face. She knew he had not even bothered to think up an alibi for himself, an excuse for being on the path at this time of day. Fool! But along with her exultation at catching him on the hop she felt her heart sink. He *was* following her; there was no chance now that he'd been here by accident, on some innocent errand.

"Got a few things to do, down at the beach," he said at last, his voice sharpened a little with anger at being caught out.

"Fishing?" she asked, with a sudden wild spurt of mockery, surveying his totally empty hands. Surely attack was the best form of defence?

"Just things," he said sullenly. "I'll walk along wi' you." And he raised an arm towards her, in a curling arc. It left her with only two choices. Either she moved off towards the sea, in the direction he wanted, or she let him touch her.

A bolder woman would have stood her ground; let the hand touch her, and greet it with an icy

64

glance, a flinch of disgust that would really put him to flight. But Rose had never had that kind of boldness, and she was aware of being alone.

She moved off towards the sea, in front of him. He was content to follow behind. It was not re-assuring. Now her backside was tingling, and the backs of her thighs. She was sure he was looking at her figure, in the nastiest possible kind of way. And it was unnerving, not being able to see him.

"There's room to walk two abreast," she said, stopping abruptly. Then was sorry for what she'd said. The word abreast contained the word "breast" and he looked at hers, now, with the slight smile of a secret joke on his face.

Still, he had to walk beside her after that, and she took care to drop back a little, so that he could no longer look at her, but she could look at him, without having to meet him eye-to-eye. And she stayed silent, trying to force him to say something. They said whoever broke a silence first was the weakest . . .

"You enjoying your grand vacation, then?"

She almost said, "Till you came along to spoil it," but bit her lip just in time. Then she just said, "Yes."

"I would have thought you would find us dull, after all the grand things you're used to . . . "

"What sort of grand things are those?"

"Foreign travel. Tunisia? Thailand?"

He was really asking where her husband was. It wouldn't do any harm to let him know she had a husband.

"My husband can't get away from his firm at the

moment. They're very busy." Then she added, "He's hoping to get down at the weekend."

"Only hopin'? He *must* be busy!"

She said, defiantly, "They *are*!" But she didn't sound convincing, even to herself.

"Can't imagine a grand businessman like your husband taking to an old dump like Sepp Yaxley's. I'd 'a' thought he'd want a five-star hotel!"

"He likes curious old things. Like me."

"I wouldn't 'a' called you a curious old thing, missus!"

They had reached the beach, and he turned and surveyed her with an up-and-down admiration that was pure insult. "So what kind of curious old things do *you* like? What do you get up to, in Richmond? What's in for the jet-set these days? Still wife-swapping down there? Or isn't that good enough any more? Black magic rituals? Witches' covens? Dancing naked on the back lawn? That's what you read in the papers . . . "

Rose could scarcely believe her ears. Rose, whose idea of a pleasant social gathering was listening to a friend's clever daughter from the Royal College of Music playing Chopin on the piano.

Her patent amazement must have pierced even his stupidity. His eyes dropped; for once, he was silent. She stared wildly at the breaking waves on the beach. Whatever had possessed him to bring up the topic of black magic?

He almost seemed to pick up her question out of the air, as if she had spoken out loud.

"It's just what you read in the papers," he said, almost humbly, as if aware he had dropped a clanger and wanting to make up for it. Or cover it up.

"I'm afraid I don't read that type of newspaper," she said frostily.

"So you *are* a reader, then? Interested in books? Old books, mebbe?"

"Jane Austen," she said. "Virginia Woolf, Iris Murdoch. Good biographies." She took a delight in the fact that he hadn't a clue what she was talking about. "Highbrow stuff," she added viciously. Put the lout in his place while you could.

But he just stared at the horizon and said, "I hear old Sepp Yaxley was a great reader . . . "

"He had a lot of books." It seemed a safer topic of conversation.

"Old Nathan Gotobed said you'd found one o' Sepp's. He saw you readin' it . . . "

God, how gossip got around in this village! So it *had* been that book that had frightened Mr. Gotobed. Well, at least she could use gossip in reverse now, to her own advantage.

"Oh, *that*," she said, with an attempt at a light laugh. "I couldn't make head nor tail of it. I just found it while I was dusting. I was curious, that's all."

He swung round to face her. "So it meant nowt to you, then?"

"Not a thing. It was in some sort of shorthand. I can't read shorthand."

"Can I borrow it? I used to be able to read shorthand. I took a bit at nightschool." His eyes, an unpleasant gooseberry colour, were suddenly avid. For the first time, she realised what he was after. And it wasn't *her*. A huge wave of relief swept over her, and with it, a little tinge of ridiculous pique.

"Oh, it wasn't that sort of shorthand. Not evening-class shorthand. I know the look of *that*."

"Look," he said fiercely. "Let me borrow it. I'll give it you back safe . . . "

"It's not mine to give. It belongs to Miss Yaxley. You'll have to ask her."

"Don't be such a fool." In his avidity he had grasped her wrist, hurting it. "You give me that book, you'll have no more bother . . . "

For once, she was able to look him in the face, as she struggled to free her wrist. What on earth did he want the book for? She was sure he wouldn't be able to read it.

"Would you mind letting go of my wrist? You're hurting me. And what do you mean, bother . . . ?" She managed to snatch her wrist free.

"You don't know this lot round here like I know them. They're like nobody you ever met. They think us London people are fools . . . they're peasants, this lot. Medieval peasants . . . " There was so much bitterness in his voice, and it was not directed at her. It was directed at the people he lived with. Maybe at the wife who could dismiss him to fetch a case of Lilt, send him away like a kicked cur. Suddenly she felt a little sorry for him, a fellow-Londoner marooned on this lonely coast.

Perhaps he saw her eyes soften. Because it made him grab her again, by both wrists this time.

"Please!" she cried. "You're *hurting*!" She struggled.

There was a slight choofing chug from somewhere on her right, somewhere inland, in the region of the last hedge. There was a hiss in the air. And the next second, Jack Sydenham's ridiculous trilby hat lifted from his head and went spinning through the air, to land six feet away on the sand.

He was so startled, he let go of her wrists. They both stared at the hat, in mutual amazement. There wasn't a breath of wind to have moved the hat so mysteriously.

Finally, Jack Sydenham took a step forward, then another, and picked the hat up.

"There's a hole in it," he said stupidly. "Two holes. One in each side."

"That'll teach you to lay hands on my mother," called a clear young voice. And there was Timothy walking down the beach, with that appalling long black air-pistol in his hand. And Jane was just behind him, fixing Jack Sydenham with her most ferocious glare.

"You young toy," roared Jack Sydenham. "That was a good hat. That was my best bloody hat. Cost me twelve quid . . . " He closed in on Timothy.

The air-pistol came up in Timothy's hand, quite unwavering. Pointing at Jack Sydenham's nose. Rose stared horrified at the black hole in the end of it; she was sure it was loaded again.

So was Jack Sydenham. At least he stopped in his tracks and changed his bluster.

"Have you got a licence for that thing? I'll have the police on you . . . "

"Please do," said Timothy. "Then I can tell them how you manhandled my mother. Common assault. If not indecent assault, eh, Jane? And three witnesses against one. You haven't got a prayer, chum.''

His eyes and Jack Sydenham's locked a long time. Then Timothy said, "I should push off, if I were you. While you still can.''

Jack Sydenham made a noise that was halfway between a yell and a groan. Then he was striding away up the path, away from the sea. Timothy watched him till he was well away, then turned and took careful aim at a can with a yellow label, lying on the sand among the seaweed, twenty yards away. The air-pistol chugged again, and the can leapt a yard in the air.

An icy hand clutched Rose's vitals. Dear God, it had been loaded! And she had seen her son's finger tighten on the trigger!

"Timothy," she said faintly.

"What?" he said, very offhanded, loading again, and closing one eye, firing and making the can jump again. And again. And again.

"Timothy, I don't think you ought to have that gun. Not till you're older.''

"Would you rather have been raped, dear little Mummy dear?''

"*Timothy*!"

"We saw him from the village," said Jane. "We saw him following you down the path. We knew he was up to no good. So we ran back to the cottage and got Tim's gun. We ran like *hell* all the way.''

Rose's heart moved within her. It was the idea of them running like hell all the way. They stared at her, young faces full of concern, and she knew suddenly how much they loved her. Traitorous tears started in her eyes, and she knew she just couldn't be stern enough to get the gun off Tim. It would be so *ungracious* to try. It would be punishing virtue, and she could never punish virtue.

"He wasn't after me," she said. "He was after Sepp Yaxley's book. The one I found. The one that upset Mr. Gotobed."

"There's something very odd about that book," said Tim, still quite cool. "I shall have to have a good close look at it. Meanwhile," he added, "Mr. Gotobed's wheelbarrow is still sitting unguarded in the middle of the village. If somebody nicks it, we are in trouble."

And the next second, to shouts of "Ta-ra" they had taken to their heels up the path.

Rose followed, very shaken all of a sudden. Full of recent memories of love and hate that swept over her like waves. Jack Sydenham's hate, her children's love. She mustn't underestimate either.

She must do something to soothe her nerves. She must do something to break the spell of this utterly strange place.

She would go and shop in Cley. It would do her good.

Six

Cley did her good at first. People said good morning in Cley, or at least nodded in a friendly way if you passed them in the street. The shopkeepers smiled and called her madam. Nobody thought her a monster. She bought yogurts and quiches and pasties and postcards of the church, and even more Coke for Mr. Gotobed, in case the kids coaxed him back.

But when she came out of the last shop, clouds had covered the sun, heavy rainclouds, though it wasn't raining yet. The dimness depressed her; she told herself she was far too vulnerable to the weather. Ever since she'd been a little girl, sunshine had meant God was smiling at her; and clouds had meant he'd turned his face away . . .

As she drove south out of the village, she saw the church lights were on, in the gloom. It reminded her that Cley church had very lovely medieval bench-ends, intricately carved, and noted in all the handbooks on Norfolk. She parked the car and told herself she would go in and inspect them; though to be truthful, she had to admit to herself she was looking for a little more than medieval oak.

The church was busy with women in pinafores, and filled with the cheering odours of Brasso and furniture polish. The chatter was not particularly godly, being mainly about the ailments of the elderly and the adultery of the young. The talk stopped as she neared, but the women smiled and bobbed their heads, as if to reassure her that she was not among the topics of conversation. She started to study the bench-ends, with great concentration, to indicate to the women what her business in their church was. Satisfied, they went back to dusting and chattering.

She was so lost in the bench-ends that the male voice startled her. "Lovely, aren't they? The best in Norfolk, they say . . . " The voice was musical and warm, south Welsh.

She turned and saw it was a little minister, very proper in clerical grey. Chubby face, and really nice smile. He looked young, with his wavy dark hair; a mere boy, except that he was going bald in front. Somehow she knew there was no danger of his going holy on her. Although she was quite religious herself, she had a horror of ministers who suddenly dragged God into a conversation by the scruff of His neck.

"You're on holiday." It was a statement, not a question.

"Yes." She smiled back; his smile was really very infectious.

"We've got a cottage at Wallney . . . "

"Wallney?" He raised dark smooth eyebrows. "Some of my ladies do a good bed-and-breakfast, but I didn't know anybody down Wallney way . . . " He gave a little frown, though it might have been only a frown of concentration.

"Miss Yaxley . . . "

"Oh, Miss *Yaxley*, yes." His face cleared. "My only stalwart in the village of Wallney, I'm afraid to say. Never misses Christmas and Easter. Otherwise, I'm afraid they're a godless lot. If they'd all been like Wallney, I think they'd have broken my heart long since." His mouth winced slightly, as if at unhappy memories.

"Why should a whole village be godless?" She felt a surge of sympathy; ministers had an uphill struggle these days.

"Oh," he shrugged. "They've never had their own church, of course. Country people are more loyal to their church than they are to God. The church is where their memories are . . . when I have an appeal for the tower or the organ or the roof, here, far more people give money than ever come to church, even for harvest festival. I think Wallney must always have resented not having its own church . . . " He went on frowning, as if there was more he hadn't said.

"But it's more than just that?" she coaxed. She liked him; and she was nosy about Wallney.

"Yes, well." He made a gesture, as if shoving something away. "There was . . . Miss Yaxley's brother. A troublesome man. Though of course I was sorry when he died," he added hastily.

"An atheist?" She had had bother with militant atheists all her life.

"No, not an atheist exactly." He seemed to come to some kind of decision. "What the old Norfolk people used to call a Cunning Man. Almost the last of them, actually. Thank God. As far as I know, that is. At least we haven't got one in Cley any more. They say, last century, there used to be one or more in every town in East Anglia. Almost like doctors. The National Health Service seems to have finished them off."

"What did they *do*?"

He shrugged. "Charmed warts . . . herbal remedies, that sort of thing. People went to them . . . "

"Father!" An irate female voice was raised from the far end of the nave. "Will you come and settle something about the altar flowers?"

"Not the damn flower-rota *again*," muttered the minister savagely under his breath. Then he gave her a bright smile, said, "So nice to have met you," and whisked away into the female huddle that, from the sound of its voices, was growing more irate by the minute.

Rose waited for him to come back. She was remembering the child in Wallney, who had asked her if she was the lady who was staying at the Cunning's house.

75

But when the flower-rota row was over, he didn't come back to her. He walked out. She wondered if he didn't want to say any more.

Then, looking at her watch, she saw it was nearly two o'clock. The kids would be starving.

She went into the kitchen, dumped her groceries and shouted, "Hallo?" There was no reply; the house's silence seemed oppressive. Where on earth could they have got to, all this time? She cursed herself for being an irresponsible mother, letting her children wander wild in a strange place, while she wallowed in the fleshpots of Cley.

But it was all right. There they were down by the outhouse; crouched on their heels, playing with something.

Something that seemed to be moving, alive. A wild thought about black rabbits in her head, she ran down the path.

But it wasn't a black rabbit; it was a cat; the cat she had met two nights ago, walking back from the village. Again she thought what an unlikeable cat it was; the massive back, the thick neck, the wedge-shaped head and dark striped coat. But it seemed to have made friends with the children. It was allowing itself to be stroked; was even extending and retracting its claws with a tiny scratching noise on the brick path, rubbing its head against Timothy's hand. But . . . stiffly, as if it was playing a part it scarcely remembered.

"I don't think you should encourage it," she said. "I'll bet that's the thing that was making the row all night. If it does it again tonight, I'll hold you responsible."

"I expect it was just lonely," said Jane. "It hasn't tried yowling since we met it."

"Did you find Mr. Gotobed?"

"We had to go to his Mum's cottage. She said he'd gone to bed and couldn't talk to us. But we showed her the wheelbarrow and said we'd come to say we were sorry, and could he still come and see to us? Then she went upstairs and nagged him something terrible, and when he came down he had his rubbers on the same as usual . . . "

"What did he say?"

"He was very jumpy. But he took us to see his vegetable garden at the back, and asked us a lot of questions about *you*."

"Me?" She got into a flurry, wondering what they must have told him. Children did say the most dreadful things about one . . .

"He asked if you ever cured our warts? And we said yes, and he asked how, and we said with some brown stuff out of a bottle that the doctor gave you. And then he asked if you ever *found* things for people. And we said just things like text-books and gym-kit for us in the mornings, and that really you were far better at losing things yourself than finding things. That seemed to cheer him up. Then he asked if you had any *books* and we said thousands and he nearly had a fit till we said they were all Dad's paperbacks and the novels that were up for the Booker Prize and all that stuff. Modern printed books. He said there were no harm in them

77

modern printed books. Then he asked about the book you were holding this morning, and we said you'd just found it and were trying to read it, but couldn't. Then he said if you promised to burn that book, he'd come back and see to us, though he wouldn't do no more gardening for you . . . "

"I can't go burning *books*." Rose's liberal soul rose up in rage. "If you start burning books, you end up burning people. Hitler burnt books. Besides," she added, "that book is the property of Miss Yaxley. I can't burn her property. Really, that man is getting above himself. There must be somebody else who can see to us, in the village . . . " But her heart failed, at the idea of asking.

"Maybe you should ask Miss Yaxley," said Tim. "If she says burn it too, you're off the hook. Go on, Mum. The outhouse's starting to smell."

Dear God, she thought, as she set off for Miss Yaxley's with the book in her hand, this is totally ridiculous. Other people are batting me around like a ping-pong ball. This has really got to *stop*.

She found Miss Yaxley gardening: crouched on an ancient garden-kneeler with all rusty handles, removing low weeds that looked as stubborn as herself from the cracks of her crazy paving. Miss Yaxley rose with a great effort to her feet; her downward pressure on the rusty handles made the kneeler quiver. Rose thought how sad it was; the garden was truly lovely, but Miss Yaxley seemed to garden without pleasure, with a grim set mouth as if she were preparing a corpse for burial in the autumn.

"What is it now?" asked Miss Yaxley, crossly. Rose knew she had long outworn any welcome.

"I came to ask you about this book I've found — it must have been one of your brother's." Rose took the book from her long cardigan pocket.

"I don't want *that*," said Miss Yaxley abruptly. "Shove it in the fire and burn the thing."

Rose was appalled at being given the same heartless advice twice. "But it's old. It might be valuable. Or of historic interest."

"You keep it then!" The words were almost spat out; never had Rose known a gift given less graciously.

"But . . . aren't you interested? He was your brother!"

"He were a pain and botheration to me all me life," said Miss Yaxley. "I don't want reminding of him." But perhaps she was not quite so hard as her words sounded. For Rose saw she was chewing her old lips, with her head right down.

"Well, thank you very much," she said gently. "I've got friends who might be interested in this book . . ."

"If you'll take my advice, you'll burn it," said Miss Yaxley. "There's a fire yonder." She nodded towards a bonfire in the corner of the garden, where she was burning a mass of leaves and garden rubbish. "You don't know what you've got there. But God has no mercy on the ignorant."

Something in her voice frightened Rose. Like an obedient small child, she walked up to the bonfire. It looked just a heap of slightly-smoking weeds, but one side had fallen in, disclosing a pile of grey ash that glowed deep red as the wind blew. She held the book out over it. But it went against the grain of all her upbringing. Her father had worshipped books and she was his child too.

Finally, after hovering a long time, she thrust the book back in her pocket. "I'll keep it, thank you. In memory of your brother."

Miss Yaxley stood staring at her garden hedge. Still she bit her lips, as if fighting against tears. It was unusually dreadful, in such a grim old woman; it was like watching a rock trying not to cry.

"He weren't a bad man," she said. "Just a meddling fool, who thought he was something he weren't. What he did, they wanted him t' do and they paid him for it. They beat a path to his front door. And then they turned agin him; those who made him do things. That child wasn't his fault. The coroner said so. But they took agin him."

"Which child? Who were *they*?"

"None o' your business. *I* told you to burn that book. It's on your head now." She shook herself, like a dog shakes off water after a swim and said, "I've got things to do." And knelt again to her weeding.

Rose dithered; and then went. There was no point in talking to that bent back; no more than there would be to a stone.

She had not been gone five minutes when an old man put his head over Miss Yaxley's hedge and said sharply, "She brought the book?"

Miss Yaxley did not look up at him. But she said, quite distinctly, "I told her to burn it. But she wouldn't. She kept it. You can't hold that against me."

That evening, when Rose went up to phone Philip, she noticed the lights were still on in the mini-market. It must be a late closing night or something.

She rang her home number. And still got the answering machine. A storm of worry and rage burst out of her like a hurricane. Philip was trying to punish her for changing his well-laid plans for her holiday. He was cutting her dead. He was trying to frighten her into rushing home like a terrified child. Well, two could play at that game! She was damned if she would rush home. Let him sweat it out as well.

Then another wave of emotion hit her, running in the opposite direction. He might be lying ill and helpless, after a heart attack. His cholesterol level had been high, in his last checkup. Or he might have fallen downstairs and broken his leg . . .

She thought of ringing the neighbours. But she didn't know the neighbours. She didn't even know their *name*.

She could ring the police; they'd check. Then she thought of all the scorn Philip would heap on her, if he was really all right. A silly woman, making a silly womanish fuss . . .

She bit her lip. She could ring him at the office in the morning. When of course she would get his secretary, the super-efficient Ms. Sampson. Who would say, with the faintest tinge of scorn, that

Philip was in some meeting, and had she a number where he could ring her back? Explaining her situation to the cool scorn of Ms. Sampson would be *very* humiliating.

In the end, she said to the answering machine that she would ring at eight the following night. She had a problem that she could do with Philip's advice on. Quite a worrying little problem! That would fetch him; like the cheese in a trap fetches the silly mouse. Philip could no more resist giving good advice than a silly mouse could resist cheese.

Quite pleased with herself, she thought she'd buy the kids a chocolate bar each, as a treat. To eat over the evening game of Scrabble. Of course it was bad for their teeth, but if they cleaned them thoroughly at bedtime it would be all right.

She walked across to the mini-market. Said good evening warmly to the round-shouldered woman with the hair on her upper lip, since the shop was otherwise empty.

The woman did not reply; did not look up from the evening paper she had spread on the counter. Rose wondered whether she was a bit deaf. So she said loudly, "Two Kit-Kat bars, please, and a tube of Smarties."

The woman still did not look up; but her right hand, as if it had a life of its own, went behind her, and lifted two Kit-Kats and a tube of Smarties off the shelf and put them on the counter. Then the hand was held out for money . . .

Rose put a pound coin into it. Silently, the pound coin was put in the till, and the change produced, and dropped on to the open newspaper. Oddly shaken, Rose scrabbled for the coins, very aware that her fingers had all turned into thumbs. Then she said "Good night" without hope; she wondered curiously what was so enthralling in the newspaper that it had made the woman so rude . . .

It appeared to be the fat stock prices at Norwich Market. She was being deliberately cut.

She walked out briskly, telling herself she had been a fool to break her resolution not to enter that shop again. The shop door closed behind her in silence.

Across the square, the single streetlamp glimmered bluely on Rose's white Golf. It looked more desolate than ever. Rose walked across, to check the doors again.

Right across the passenger door was scrawled one word. Very large and very jagged and violent, in the thin layer of road-dirt.

The word was

WITCH

Rose stared and stared at it. She wished it had been some other word, like "Bitch" or even "Fuck." A word that belonged to the real if sinful world. But this was a word that nobody ever used, unless they were reading some silly book to children. Yet somehow, on her own car door in the dim lamplight, the word did not look silly at all. It looked as real as the word "Yuppie." And the venom in the strokes . . .

Rose took out her handkerchief and smeared the word out. She could not bear it to exist in her world. She rubbed and rubbed long after the word was gone; until the door was shiny and clean as the day she had bought the car.

Then she thought she was a fool. She had just shown to the village that she had read the word; and that it had upset her into ruining with black dirt a perfectly good hanky.

She set off at a brisk pace for the cottage, aware that the eyes of the woman in the shop were following her all the way. And how many other eyes, behind the curtains of the village? By the time she reached the cottage, she was running.

And yet how silly it all seemed, as she opened the kitchen door. Curtains drawn against the dark, oil-lamps lit, the fire well made up and casting everything in a rosy glow. The kitchen table laid for Scrabble . . .

The two kids sitting peacefully in the rockers each side of the range, rocking, with their feet up on the fender, a picture of contentment.

And on Jane's knee, the cat.

"I told you not to encourage that animal," she snapped.

They looked at her with open mouths; she had never been a snapper.

"It's lost and hungry," said Jane. "We gave it a pasty and it ate the lot, even the pastry and crumbs."

"People have tried to shoot it," said Timothy. "It has all little scars on one side and a shotgun pellet came out of one when I picked it. The people round here must be *beastly*."

The cat continued to purr and knead on Jane's knee. But it gave Rose a wary, calculating look, an old cold look. It knew it had won two hearts, but not three.

And yet its wounds won it the day.

"Yes," said Rose, "the people round here are rather beastly, I'm afraid."

"Even Mr. Gotobed," said Timothy, with the sudden crushing condemnation of the young. "We've been thinking about it. We don't think he set those snares to catch a rabbit. We think he set them to try and catch the cat. Those hairs I found round the snare weren't rabbit-hairs, they were hairs from the cat. There aren't any rabbits round here. There isn't a trace of droppings."

"But why would he want to catch the cat?" asked Rose. "What had it done to him?" She was reluctant to cast Mr. Gotobed as a villain, along with the rest.

"Because the cat was digging in our garden, I suppose. Cos if there are no rabbits, the cat must have dug those holes down by the outhouse."

"But cats don't dig burrows," said Rose, a bit feebly.

"They do to bury their cr — droppings," said Jane, with a last-minute swerve of voice.

"Oh, I suppose so," said Rose. "Though what damage a cat could do to a hopeless garden like this . . . "

"I expect Mr. Gotobed had grand new plans for it," said Timothy. "Like that stupid rockery of his."

"You mustn't be rude about him," said Rose hastily. "The outhouse . . . "

"Oh, we won't be rude to him," said Jane. "We'll be *polite* for your sake. But we're not friends of his any more . . . "

Rose shuddered. Mr. Gotobed was out in the freezing wastes now. She hoped she was never sent to join him.

"Oh, I suppose the cat can stay. If it behaves itself," she added. It wasn't just that she wanted the children's approval. She felt . . . beleaguered now, and the cat became a comrade in misfortune. When they went, they'd take the cat with them, if it wanted to come, leave this horrible village. They could find it a good home, even if Philip put his foot down about keeping it. A little glow lit up in her, a mischievous little glow. Let Philip try fighting the kids about getting rid of the cat. That might cut him down to size a bit . . .

Really, she told herself severely, I'm turning into a not very nice person.

"Scrabble," she said briskly.

Jane got up, and carefully replaced the cat on her rocker. It turned round and round about six times, then settled with a satisfied look on its face. Almost as if it lived here . . .

It was not a very good game of Scrabble. At least for Rose. Visions kept drifting through her mind. Miss Yaxley's grim tormented face; tears gathering in the corners of its stoniness, as if Moses had smote the rock and water came forth. The silence of the woman in the shop, the coldness of rejection. The scrawl on the car door . . . the little minister's doubtfulness.

"Poor old Mum's off form," said Timothy smugly at the end. "Me 197, you 192 Jane, Mum 109."

"How's Daddy?" asked Jane, with careful casualness.

"How's the answering machine," said Rose with feeling.

"Poor old Mum," said Timothy, pouring the Scrabble tiles back into the bag that held them. "You don't think he's having an affair with Ms. Sampson, do you, Mum?" He asked with only the mildest interest.

"Don't be stupid, Timothy," said Jane. "Dad's got more sense than that. If he got mixed up with Ms. Sampson, the whole firm would fall apart. Daddy's in love with his computer . . . "

"You mean he switches Ms. Sampson off when he goes home at night," said Tim.

They both giggled.

Seven

Rose came up out of sleep in a sweating panic, to the sound of the yowling. It filled the house. She desperately told herself that it was just that damned cat . . .

But the yowling was so drear, so full of doom that it asked the question what *was* a cat? A cat was a wild animal that pretended to be a tame pussy for purposes of its own. A cat was a creature without mercy, that killed live rabbits and tore them to pieces. A cat was a thing that she had once seen swallow a mouse whole, like a Smartie, head-first, while it was still alive and its back legs wriggling. A cat was eyes that knew and would not tell. Claws and jaws that would rip without . . .

She leapt out of bed, and ran to the door, stubbing her toe against the bed-leg in the dark and nearly going full-length.

Timothy opened her door, as she recovered her balance. He looked calm and collected as usual;

she had the absurd idea he had actually combed his hair. All this she saw by the light of his large torch.

"*Your* damned cat!" she shouted at him, most unfairly.

"Let's see what it's up to," he said with a cheerful consoling grin. He could be so *sweet* . . .

They blundered down the stairs, he guiding her feet with the flicking beam of the torch, and giving her instructions to be careful in a voice that was the echo of Philip's. Their flurry was made greater by the sound of a great clawing and rending.

"What is it *doing*?" she screeched.

The beam of the torch showed them. Quite impervious to the bright light, the cat was throwing itself at the closed door of the sitting-room. Like a mad thing. The thumps it was making were horrendous. It didn't seem to care if it was hurting itself or not. And the faded brown paintwork of the door showed the white weals of massive claw-damage.

"Get the thing out of the house. It's mad. It must have rabies or something." She went to the front door and flung it open on the dark cool night. Then she rushed at the cat making shooing noises.

The cat took no notice at all. It might as well have been stone deaf. Only when she grabbed it did it notice her.

She wished it hadn't. She had a brief feel of tight-strung muscles under the dark fur, of enormous cruel strength and diabolical ferocity, and then there was a spat and a flash of teeth and she reeled back clutching a hand that was agony. All feelings of pity for animals left her. This was an enemy, a demon, a devil. In a blind rage, she looked round for a weapon. And in the hall-stand, absurdly, she saw an old 1930s tennis-racket. She grabbed it and swung back and flailed at the cat. And hit it.

There was a scatter of claws on the lino, and suddenly it wasn't around any more.

"Where did it go?" she said, feeling blood running down her hand and hearing it drip on to the linoleum, somewhere in the darkness.

"Dunno," said Tim thoughtfully. "You shouldn't have hit it, Mum. It wasn't doing you any harm."

"That's what you think. Shine your torch here. I'm frightened of getting blood on this nightdress."

By the light of the torch, she held her bleeding hand over the sink. Thinking with a dreary bleakness that if the cat did have rabies, she was a goner. How would Philip manage without her? What would happen to the children? They said rabies was a hideous painful death . . .

Tim worked the water-pump, and she held her hand under its pulsing jet. The blood dwindled to two small puncture-marks; but it if was rabies, that wouldn't be any consolation.

"Keep pumping," said Timothy, managing to light an oil-lamp one-handed, while he held the torch with the other. "I'll check where it's gone. I think it went out but . . . "

Jane came trailing downstairs, half asleep, demanding to know what the hell was going on, and didn't they know what time it was? But she brightened up when she saw Rose's wounds. Went all practical and motherly, and put on TCP from the first aid kit they always carried on holiday, and slapped on two Elastoplasts. Rose felt a little calmer; she might have rabies, but at least there was no blood on her nightdress . . .

"Think it's gone, Mum," said Timothy thundering back downstairs. "I checked under all the beds."

"Let's get back to bed then, for goodness' sake," said Jane, suddenly sleepy again, now the blood had departed, and all the thrills were over.

But I've got rabies, thought Rose. I ought to summon the doctor. But that would mean getting dressed and walking up to the car, and phoning, and getting the car started . . . it seemed less bother to go back to bed and die of rabies quietly. She shut the front door and went back to bed, starting to plan the making of her will, so as not to cause needless bother to Philip after she was gone. Jane would have her jewellery, but not till she was twenty-one. She didn't want her own grandmother's pearls to end up round Jane's neck at some Acid House rave-up . . .

She was just dozing off, having left Philip her Swift Audubon binoculars, with the sincere hope that he would derive peace and consolation from them, when the uproar broke out downstairs anew.

Again, she flung herself out of bed and stubbed her toe on the bed-leg, and nearly went flying.

Her bedroom door opened more quickly this time. A torch-lit Timothy said, "Leave it to me this time, Mum!" Obediently, she followed him downstairs. He stood watching the frenzy of the cat, his head on one side. Then he said, judiciously, "I don't think it's got rabies, Mum. It just wants to get into the sitting-room." And he walked across and opened the sitting-room door.

Immediately the cat calmed down, and slipped through the dark slit. And then, in the darkness, the terrible clawing started again. Timothy pushed the door wider, and shone the torch.

The beam caught the cat on its hind legs.

It was clawing at the tall locked cupboard beside the fireplace. Its whole body quivering with alertness, ears pricked for the slightest sound.

As if there was somebody hiding behind the cupboard door.

Rose's world rocked anew; with all thought of rabies forgotten. The cupboard was as tall as a man. The wall it was set in, the outside wall of the cottage, could be three feet thick. There could be a man standing in there. A big old man, come back to claim his own.

The cat mewed, as if in dreadful greeting; its tail lashed wildly from side to side. Rose thought of secret passages underground, of tunnels and crypts. Oh, what rubbish you could think at two o'clock in the morning!

"There's something in that cupboard," said Jane behind her. "Something the cat *wants*."

Rose wished Jane had not said "thing." "Thing" was dead. Rose had a terrible vision of the seven-year-old corpse of Sepp Yaxley, propped upright behind that well-clawed door, waiting to fall out upon the first person to open it. Somehow, Sepp

92

Yaxley dead was worse than Sepp Yaxley living. Or returned from the grave . . .

The cat mewed dreadfully, yearningly again. Who can know the minds of dumb beasts? And then Rose summoned common sense to her aid. The police would have searched the cottage, surely, when Sepp Yaxley first disappeared? Or would they, if they thought he'd been drowned on the marshes? Suppose he had stepped inside the cupboard and the heavy door slammed shut on him, like that girl in the old poem of her youth who hid in the clothes-chest on her wedding-night, and was found a skeleton years later?

"I think we'd better open that cupboard, Mum!" said Timothy judiciously. "At least it will settle the cat's mind, and we can get back to bed." But there was a wild flick of excitement in his voice that disturbed her.

"How can we open it?" she snapped. "It's locked and we haven't got a key!"

"I can pick the lock, easy," said Timothy. "Jonathan Stephens showed me how, last holidays. We practised picking the locks on his father's car. I'll just get my Swiss knife."

Rose sat down weakly, and wondered what the world was coming to. Her terror of the cupboard was suddenly and irrationally displaced by a fear for her son's criminal future . . .

His feet thundered downstairs again. They all waited now, in silence. Even the cat, which seemed to have realised that aid was at hand; though it still mewed urgently, every few seconds, with one paw pitifully uplifted in expectation.

Timothy selected a long thin blade from the hundreds on the Swiss knife. "Come and hold the torch, Mum," he said. "No, steadier than that. Use both your hands!"

"Oh, come on, *I'll* do it," said Jane, taking the torch from her. "You're a proper wet lettuce, Mum."

Rose sat down again. She would never understand the rising generation. They seemed so utterly heartless. Without feeling. Only concerned with how much is it? Or, is there a quick kick in it? Debunking, cynical, on to the next cheap thrill.

Nor could she understand her own cowardice. Sitting at a safe distance while her two children were about to be fallen on by a long-dead corpse, a member of the living dead, or even a vampire . . .

The knife scrawped; the lock clicked. The tall door swung open, sending a great shadow as of death sweeping across the torchlit room.

And there was a smell, a dusty smell, a sweet smell, a sour smell, an infinitely evil smell.

"Oh," said Jane, her voice sagging in disappointment. "Just jars. Books and jars. All that fuss over a few books and jars . . . "

"This one's got frogs in," said Timothy hopefully. "Dead frogs."

"We've got those in the bio lab at school," said Jane dismissively. "Anyway, they're toads."

"And there's newts," said Timothy. "And I think those are animals' eyes . . . " Hope of horrors still lingered in his voice.

"I don't like biology, it's yuk," said Jane. "We had to dissect a frog at school and mine was a

94

female full of eggs. I spent a whole morning scraping out the eggs, and then we had tapioca for school dinner . . . I'm off to bed. Have a nice supper! It's *lovely* having a kinky brother . . . "

"Who says I'm kinky?"

"Half the girls in my class. I've had *fights* with girls who called you kinky. I needn't have bothered. They're *right*." She blundered away into the dark, tripping on one of the middle stairs in the process, and saying something that in happier circumstances Rose would have found quite unforgivable.

"Ey, Mum," said Tim, grasping for a new ally. "There's some jolly odd stuff in here. I think there's a baby in one of these jars . . . "

"Oh, what rubbish," said Rose, starting forward. "Really, Tim, you're quite *impossible*."

"No, look!"

Reluctantly, she went forward. In the light of his torch, the dead frogs, frozen in the act of leaping, in their prison bath of dirty formalin, looked at her appealingly, still yearning for freedom and life outside the jar. The newts looked more reconciled to their fate, grim and nearly asleep. But the creature in the black jar, with its bulging forehead and never-opened eyes, its tiny budlike arms and legs . . .

"It must be a chimpanzee fetus or something," said Rose desperately.

"Go on," said her son heartlessly. "It's *human*. The Sunday supplements are full of them. I wonder where he got it?"

"I think we ought to go to bed," said Rose. It

was the only sensible thought she could pluck from her churning mind.

Her son eyed her acutely. In the upward light of the torch, he looked . . . unearthly. Like a . . . not a devil, but a rather scary angel. Beautiful, and yet . . . unknowable, with his high forehead and large observant eyes. It had never occurred to her before that angels like Michael and Gabriel could be a bit scary. But after all, they had to put down devils, trample them under their feet . . .

"He was a funny old bloke, Mum, wasn't he? Sepp Yaxley, I mean. I wonder what *really* happened to him . . . "

"Bed," said Rose firmly. It took some courage, after what she'd been through, to say "bed" firmly to an avenging angel. So they went to bed; and that other avenging angel, the cat, was nowhere to be seen.

Eight

Contrary to her expectations of nightmares about frogs and embryos, Rose slept the dreamless sleep of a log, and stumbled downstairs next morning, feeling half-dead. She found the kids, perversely, in excellent spirits, sitting by the window in the sunshine, Jane with the cat in her lap. The devil of the night before gave her a wary look. It obviously had not forgotten the tennis-racket. But Jane went on stroking it, and said, rather meaningfully, "It's all right, puss. Mum didn't mean it. She's quite *nice* really."

Timothy said to the cat, "It's the first time she's hit anything with a tennis-racket for ages. You're quite safe."

"My hand's throbbing. Where it bit me," said Rose, hurt at all the sympathy going one way.

"You'd better get to the doctor's straight away," said Jane briskly. "And have injections."

97

"Oh, it's nothing," said Rose. "I don't want to bother the doctor. He'll be busy."

"If it was one of us," said Timothy darkly, "you'd have taken us already. What if you have got rabies? Or tetanus? How could we look after you? Who would drive us home?"

Cursing them for a hard-faced lot, Rose went reluctantly, after breakfast. She inspected the car carefully for further graffiti, on the pretext of checking the doors and tires. There did not appear to be anything new; though she thought one or two curtains twitched, in the nearer houses.

The doctor turned out to be an elderly woman, who was not at all sympathetic.

"How on earth did you manage to let yourself be bitten by a *cat*?" She made Rose feel like a shambolic fifth-former, as she listened in stony silence while Rose stammered through an explanation.

"Never heard anything so ridiculous in my life," she said, when Rose finally stumbled to a stop. "Encouraging stray cats into your house . . . "

"It's not my house," said Rose feebly. "It's a holiday cottage. The cat might have lived there . . . "

"Surely you were told whether the cat lived there or not? And whoever heard of a cat living in a *holiday* cottage? You city folk are innocents abroad. What holiday cottage is this? I think I'll ring up the RSPCA. That cat is a *menace*."

"No, no," said Rose, terrified that the cat was about to be condemned to death by her own foolish mouth. "I'm sure Miss Yaxley knows about it . . . "

"Nora Yaxley? Nora Yaxley can't stand cats. Never had a cat in her life."

"It's not at Miss Yaxley's. It's at her brother's old cottage."

"*Sepp* Yaxley's cottage?" The doctor's tone had changed subtly, in a way that made Rose forget her humiliation and prick up her ears.

"Did you know Sepp Yaxley?"

The doctor stared down at her desk, as if some errant Biro had wandered out of its rightful place, and was about to be hammered to fragments for its impudence. "I knew Sepp Yaxley," she said in a cold stony voice. "I was gathering evidence that would have sent him to prison. Only the evidence was difficult to get, and he . . . died, before I was ready to go to the police."

"What for?" gasped Rose, aghast. "What had he done?"

"Young girls," said the doctor, and then clamped her mouth shut like a rat-trap. Then she got up and said, "It's water under the bridge now, anyway. And it's best not to speak ill of the dead, though I'm half inclined to make an exception in the case of Sepp Yaxley. Well, no doubt he's gone to his reward. Meanwhile, I think we'll give you a couple of jabs. All cats have filthy mouths, and we don't want you going down with something nasty in your *charming* country cottage."

She turned away to a shelf of medicines and syringes, and added to herself, under her breath, something that sounded to Rose like, "Nora Yaxley must be out of her senses. Senile decay setting in, I wouldn't wonder."

Rose suffered two exceptionally painful jabs, as if she was being punished for her sins.

Driving out of Cley, she saw her little minister raising his hat to two lady parishioners as he came out of the newspaper shop, a copy of the *Independent* under his arm. She was so glad to see a friendly face that she drew into the curb and waited till he overtook her. She wound down the passenger window.

"Can you spare a minute, vicar?"

"Certainly, my dear!" He got in alongside her. "How are you, this lovely morning? Still enjoying your holiday?"

She took one look at his smiling face, and a dam seemed to burst inside her. She poured out her whole tale of woe, feeling terribly guilty to be wiping the smile off his face, and blighting his morning.

When she'd finally ground to a halt, he bit his lip and said, "I wish you'd told me before. That it was Sepp Yaxley's cottage she was renting to you. It never occurred to me she'd rent out *that* place. But she's a hard woman, Nora Yaxley. She'll have her rights if it kills her. I suppose she thought you were too good a chance to miss, being a stranger who hadn't a clue. And I suppose she took a chance on your being honest . . . well, she got what she wanted. Sepp's valuables, without having to bribe somebody to clear Sepp's house."

100

"But she could have walked down any time and collected Sepp's things . . . "

The minister sighed, and was silent a long time, watching the house martins feeding their young under the eaves of the nearby house, back and forth, back and forth.

At last he said reluctantly, "You'll find this difficult to believe; but people have been terrified of that house. Any Cunning Man's house. It used to be the same all over East Anglia. There's a bit in a book by Richard Deacon, about a man who lived on the Suffolk border — Cunning Murrell was his name. There were all sorts of tales told about Cunning Murrell — he's supposed to have lived to be well over a hundred. They say he could charm wild hares in the field — that they'd come and eat out of his hand. But the real point is that when he died, they could find no one who would clear out his house, for any amount of money. They had to wait months until they could persuade his son, Buck Murrell, to come and clear the house, and he came halfway across the country to do it. I suppose he must have been another Cunning Man . . . "

"But what did they do, these Cunning Men, to make people so scared of them?"

The minister shrugged. "What the country people wanted them to do. A lot of it was harmless — charming warts — anyone can charm warts, I've done it myself. And herbal remedies — useful for poor people in the time before the NHS. Finding things that people had mislaid — telling them where to look for them . . . " He trailed off again.

101

"That sounds harmless enough," said Rose stoutly. "I don't see what there is to be scared of in *that*."

"No," said the vicar. "But there were other things. Putting a blight on people's crops . . . yes. I know it sounds ridiculous, but there was a lot of that until quite recently, especially round the time of village prize vegetable shows . . . "

"God, how spiteful . . . and how childish!"

"I'd believe anything of that Wallney lot. They're just not part of the twentieth century. As they say here in Cley, one road into Wallney, and the same road out. And the inbreeding . . . they say there are only five faces in Wallney; the same faces recur time and again. Mind you, I think Cley folk have a down on Wallney. It's sort of bottom of the heap."

"That doesn't excuse them shooting at that cat . . . "

"Cats? They do it to people, let alone cats. One of my young lads here was foolish enough to try to go courting a Wallney girl. A gang of Wallney youths set on him, half-killed him and chased him out of the village. Burnt his motorbike into the bargain. He took the hint — married a Cley girl."

"Didn't the police . . . "

The minister shook his head sadly. "The policeman here knew he'd never get to the bottom of it. Wallney people stick together. They all tell the same story . . . there was nothing he could do."

"But why pick on a *cat*?"

"Oh, they'd think nothing of killing a cat. Shove

it in a bag and throw it in a pool — cat and kittens. Farmers aren't sentimental."

"Yes, but to take the trouble to *shoot* it . . . "

He was silent an even longer time, watching the house martins and scuffing his little highly polished shoes on the car's floor-covering. Then he said, "Sepp Yaxley had a cat — a striped cat. They said it disappeared the same time as he did. They might think, down Wallney, it was the same cat."

"After seven years?"

"Cats live a lot longer than seven years. When they took against Sepp, they took against the cat. There was a lot of stupid talk." He stopped again, abruptly. But she had to know.

"What kind of stupid talk?"

"Oh, ridiculous stuff . . . medieval. They said the cat was Yaxley's familiar spirit. A thing that took the form of a cat, to go about and wreak havoc. It's unbelievable how stupid they can be." He tapped his hand on the dashboard of the car. "Look, Nora Yaxley has been very naughty. She's not liked in Wallney, and she's used you to get her way, and the dirt's landed on you. It's not your fault, but you'll never get them to believe that. Why not just get out of the place? Now? It's just not your problem. If you're stuck for a place to stay, I'm sure my wife can put you up for the night, while you make other arrangements. I'll come with you now if you like, and help you to clear out your stuff . . . "

A chill went through her, at the worried look on his face. She had a great urge to take him up on his offer. It would make things so simple . . . Wallney was a miserable hole. There were dozens of nicer places in Norfolk. Almost anywhere was nicer than Wallney . . .

And then her stubborn streak surfaced. She had just escaped from a man who ran her life for her, as if she was an incompetent. And within five days, here was another arrogant male doing just the same thing, all over again. I am *not* a child, she told herself. I am *not* incompetent. If I have problems, I can solve them myself. If I can't, it's about time I grew up.

This man was nicer than Philip, more caring, more gentle. But it was the same old damned male arrogance, the same certainty that they could run the world to perfection . . .

"Thank you," she said. "You're very kind. But I'm sure I can manage."

He got out of the car, a little huffily. He closed the door with a tiny slam of criticism. Then he opened it again and said, "Be very careful what you do. They will *always* take things the wrong way. Anything outsiders do."

Then he closed the door again, and strode briskly away. Leaving her feeling rather lonely.

As she approached Wallney, her courage began to evaporate. Something deep inside her, not heard for a long time, began insisting that she pack and get out. It nagged and nagged and nagged, until she almost hit a passing car, through not looking what she was doing.

Suddenly, irrationally, she wanted to hear Philip's voice. Philip's strong certain no-nonsense voice, that would blow away in a trice all these dark cold thoughts that were invading her. She pulled up by the phone-box in the village, and looked in her purse for change.

Damn. She had nothing but notes. She would have to get change at the shop, the hostile shop.

She took herself in charge, and read herself a lecture. It was only a shop, like any other shop. It sold things. For profit. It had a living to make. It was her obedient servant. Going in to the shop would be a first step to becoming a more confident Rose. It was time she toughened up; grew a thicker skin.

She got out of the car, and locked it decisively. Strode across the square with a dominant mannish no-nonsense stride that would leave them in no doubt, as they watched her come, that she meant business.

The shop bell gave a sharp ting. But nobody in the shop took any notice. Not a head turned, though she knew they knew it was her. She pushed through them. Of course, she wouldn't just ask for change for a five-pound note. She would buy something, anything.

"Three cans of Coke!" she said briskly; at the same time realising they had enough Coke at the house already to float a battleship.

The woman looked at her, hard. There seemed to be a little gloating glint in her eye.

"I'm afraid I can't serve you, madam."

"Can't serve me? Whyever not?" Rose couldn't help her voice squeaking upwards with surprise.

"No reason."

"That's just stupid!"

"I'll thank you to keep your insults to yourself, madam. It is not the policy of this shop to serve you."

"But you have to serve me! It's against the law for you not to serve me!"

"We can serve who we like. And not serve who we don't like."

For a wild angry second, Rose had thoughts of returning with a policeman and demanding her legal rights. Then she thought perhaps she had no legal rights.

"Oh, come on, be sensible." She heard an unwelcome note of desperate pleading in her voice.

"It's within my *legal* rights, not to serve trouble-makers!" The woman was smiling now; it was not a nice smile, and Rose had an idea that she was sharing it with the others in the shop, behind Rose's back. Rose's mind shot from pleading to rage. She was being put down with drunken teenagers, and children who shoplifted.

"*How* am I a trouble-maker?" The moment she said, it, she knew it was a mistake.

The woman looked at her even more gloatingly, as if assessing which words would cause most pain. She really took her time; Rose felt inwardly frozen by such exultant cruelty.

"You come here, with your big car, and all your money that you haven't lifted a finger to earn, and you stay where you're not wanted, and poke and pry into what doesn't concern you and you plague decent law-abiding people. What respectable woman dresses up like a teenage kid? Mutton dressed as lamb? Well it might do for your grand friends up London, but it doesn't wash with folks down here. Get back to where you belong."

There was a sort of low growl of approval from the customers. Rose didn't even dare look round. She was surrounded by a massive wall of monumental ignorance and stupidity. It drove her mad; and at the same time to the verge of tears. The trouble was, she was used to always being loved, or at least liked, or at the very worst ignored.

"Oh, go to hell the lot of you!" she shouted, before she could stop herself. "I hope you all roast in hell." It was a thing she had once heard her father shout, many many years ago. It was the one thing that came into her mind; she had never felt the need for rude words since then.

There was a long profound silence in the shop. As if the people were digesting carefully what she had said, and waiting nastily for her to go on. They were so much together, so hard and unrelenting. Rose hated such people so much; she thought them the cause of all the trouble in the world.

She turned and walked out, her head held high. But she could not bear to leave them to their triumphant gossip afterwards. She turned a last time to their impervious faces, wanting to hurt as she had been hurt, and said, "You're nothing but a bunch of ignorant pigs, ignorant Norfolk pigs. You'll be sorry for this!"

And with that meaningless, pointless threat, she left.

Nine

She walked into the cottage with a face like thunder. The children were not in the kitchen; but she heard voices from the sitting-room. What the hell were they up to now?

When she opened the door, an appalling sight greeted her. The door of the cupboard was wide open, and the shelves were nearly empty. Every chair, table and flat surface was decked out with the contents of the cupboard. On the centre table, the awful embryo in the glass jar took up pride of place, surrounded by the jars of newts and toads. There were pots and bags of odd stuff scattered everywhere.

Timothy was holding one bag; he took his nose out of it as she glared at him.

"Smell this powder, Mum! It smells ever so weird."

"What the hell do you think you're doing? Put that stuff back *instantly*!"

"We were only having a nosy," said Jane. "The cat wanted to have another nosy, so we thought we'd have one." The cat was contentedly clutched in her arms.

"Put it all back this instant," Rose screamed.

"Careful, little Mumsy," said Timothy, mock-threateningly. "Or we'll turn *you* into a frog!" Holding the bag in one hand he moved glowering towards her. "Or a *slug*. And then feed you on slug-pellets." He began to gesture in the air, and then made a sign with two fingers that he'd learnt on a trip to Italy, which was either a sign for warding off the evil eye, or the sign for putting it on somebody; she couldn't quite remember.

She grabbed the bag off him and said, "Stop it, you little devil . . . "

And at that moment, she sensed the light from the open window darken. Heard an elderly voice begin. "I've seen to the . . . missus. That's all right now — "

She turned and saw Mr. Gotobed standing there. Mr. Gotobed stopped in mid-sentence. His tombstone mouth fell open. She watched his eyes widen and swivel. From the open cupboard to the embryo on the table, amidst its circle of the dead. From the gesture that Timothy was making to the bag in her own hand. And on to the striped cat that was lying purring with delight in Jane's arms . . .

Their total damnation grew on Mr. Gotobed's stupid old face. He gave a whimper, like a baby. Began to edge away from the window.

"Mr. Gotobed, I can explain everything," she

109

wailed. And then despairingly, "Mr. Gotobed, *wait*!"

But already he was a frantically bobbing head above the hedge, on his desperate way down to the village.

"What the hell did you think you were doing?" she said wearily, putting the last horrible object back in the cupboard, and slamming the door shut as if that very act of will would undo the damage.

"Looking for . . . " said Timothy.

"Treasure," said Jane defiantly. "And we found it." She dangled a worn leather bag with a draw-string defiantly under Rose's nose. "Tim says they're sovereigns, and worth about a hundred and fifty pounds each. Will we get a reward off Miss Yaxley for finding them?"

"There's a hundred and five in that bag," said Tim. "That's over fifteen thousand pounds. Finders usually get ten per cent. I'm going to buy a new mountain bike with mine."

"And I'm buying a combined colored television and VHF radio from Dixon's," added Jane.

Their eyes glowed with covetousness. For a moment, Rose felt truly scared of them. Damn them! Damn Miss Yaxley and her stupid brother who did nothing but make trouble! Damn the cat, damn this whole place, damn, damn, damn!

"There's another *book*, too," said Timothy. "And you can *read* this one." He tossed it to her, saying regretfully, "There's no magic spells. It's only an account-book . . . "

She caught it, and it fell open as it came into her

hands. And there it was, full and real, in Sepp Yaxley's crabbed handwriting:

> To charming a wart for M.J.   Two
> pounds
> To B.S. for a mixture to cure his
> back   Two pounds
> To finding Miss A.M.'s purse   Five
> pounds

But there was worse to come:

> To putting a blight on N.P.'s beans
> Five pounds
> To taking off the blight from N.P.'s
> beans   Ten pounds

The old thief, not even honest in his foul witchcraft. Taking one man's money to blight, and another's to take the blight off.

And there was one thing that was worse still.

> To curing Mrs. L.C. of her child
> Thirty pounds

She shut the book. She felt very sick.

She made lunch for the children, her hands moving automatically. She couldn't eat any herself. Things whirled round inside her head, out of control.

While she washed up, she made up her mind. She would go and have things out with Miss Yaxley, once and for all. And then they would get out of this horrible place for good.

The children were down the garden again, playing with the cat. She called to them.

"Going up to see Miss Yaxley. Won't be long. Stay close to the house, and don't do *anything*!"

They nodded absently. They had heard her; but, she suspected, only as one hears the irritating buzzing of a fly on a window. "Don't do anything. Don't touch anything," she shouted again. Timothy waved an idle lordly hand.

As she turned out of the ruined gate, she saw ahead the bent figure of an old man. He seemed to be working on the hedge that bordered the next field. Laying it, as Mr. Gotobed would have said. But he had none of the terrible hacking vigour of Mr. Gotobed. He flailed weakly, and often the result of his hacking was little more than a shower of severed leaves. Poor old thing, having to work at his age, and in his arthritic state. As she drew nearer, the sound of his puffing wheezing breathing came to her through the still air. Her heart filled with pity for him.

"Good afternoon," she greeted him with extra warmth. He glanced up at her, from his bent position. And all pity froze inside her. He had an absolutely expressionless face; a face of red-veined marble; and his dull green eyes were as cold as stones. She felt she might as well have said good morning to the expressionless eyes of a basking lizard.

Then he dropped his head again, and went on

feebly working; the sound of his gasps growing in volume.

A hundred yards on, she turned to look back at him. He had stopped work, and was standing with his elbows on the top of a nearby gate, his huge sharp billhook in his hand.

She was quite sure he was watching her house. That laying the hedge was simply an excuse, however sharp and murderous his billhook had been.

Suddenly, she felt uneasy about leaving the children alone. She hastened her steps. She must deal with Miss Yaxley quickly, and get back.

She went round the back way into Miss Yaxley's. There was no sign of the old lady in the back garden; though the garden kneeler still lay there, with a trug of weeds and a knife beside it. The weeds were old and withered; the blade of the knife was rusted with overnight dew. It made her more uneasy; Miss Yaxley was not one to forget, and leave a good knife out to rust.

She knocked on the back door. No answer, though it swung open under her knocking. She put her head round the door, and shouted "Yoohoo" as she had done so long ago, at her granny's. Then jumped with shock.

Against the dim light of the lace-curtained window, Miss Yaxley was sitting in her chair, as still as a stone. Her head did not turn; her body did not move.

Oh God, thought Rose, a stroke, a heart attack. She moved across trembling and took hold of Miss Yaxley's hand as it lay in her lap. It was very cold.

The certainty of the presence of death closed in on Rose like a cold shroud; a still agony inside a shroud of calm.

So it came as an even more dreadful shock when Miss Yaxley did move her head; when she opened her eyes. When she opened her old wrinkled lips feebly and no sound came out.

"Are you all right?" squeaked Rose. "What's happened?"

"Cold," said Miss Yaxley. "Cold."

Rose looked wildly round. There was a heavy velvet cloth on the table. She whipped it off, and tucked it round Miss Yaxley's shoulders and across her knees, lifting the cold hands one after the other and laying them on top.

The fire in the grate was cold white ash, long beyond reviving. But there was a worn greasy fan-heater lying in the corner. Rose pulled it out to Miss Yaxley's feet, and pressed the switch. To her relief, it came on with an ancient chirruping whirr. Real heat came out, dry and oppressive, but welcome to her hand.

"Cup of tea," she said to Miss Yaxley loudly. "I'll make you a cup of tea." She found the kettle and blundered about, looking for tea, sugar, milk in the strange kitchen and eventually finding them, slowed up by the constant glances in Miss Yaxley's direction. The kettle boiled, she made the tea, and took it across to Miss Yaxley. Put it on the table beside her, and took and chafed old cold hands.

"What happened, Miss Yaxley?"

The old bleary eyes looked at her emptily. The

old lips moved, with their pathetic fringe of stray hairs.

"They broke my winders," she said. And began to cry silently, the tears coursing down the wrinkled cheeks.

Rose whirled. The windows of the kitchen looked intact. But the room was cold, full of draughts coming under the door. She went and opened the door into the sitting-room, and gasped in disbelief.

Every pane in the windows had been systematically broken, from top to bottom. All Miss Yaxley's polished precious things lay under a blizzard of broken glass. From room to room she went. Every room was the same. It was more horrible than a death.

She swept back to Miss Yaxley, full of rage.

"Who's done this? We must ring the police!"

Miss Yaxley shook her head, her old eyes wide with terror.

"Not police! Make it worse!"

"It's those bloody villagers, isn't it?"

Miss Yaxley nodded. "Don't ring the police," she whispered again.

"Why ever not?" Indignation and disbelief boiled up in Rose.

"I have to live with them. In the village." The old voice was stronger now. The old hand reached for the mug of tea at her elbow, feebly. Rose picked it up and helped her drink, as if she were a child.

"They'll just say . . . it was motorbike vandals.

I didn't see who did it. I was dozing in the chair. They stick together . . . "

"You can't stay here now," said Rose, firmly but tenderly.

The old lady nodded her head in agreement.

"You should be in hospital . . . "

"No, not hospital." The fear of hospital was as vivid in the old eyes as the fear of the glass-breakers.

"Where, then?"

"Sister . . . Sheringham. Go there."

"Is she on the phone?"

Nod.

"What's her number?"

The phone, an old-fashioned black model, lay on a tiny table in the corner. Rose seized it, and was glad to hear the dialling tone. And to get Miss Yaxley's sister, who sounded at least as old as Miss Yaxley, but had all her marbles.

"No," said Rose reassuringly. "I don't think she's had a stroke or anything. She's just had a bad shock with vandals. Can she come and stay with you for a bit?"

Miss Yaxley, a little recovered in spirit, raised her legs and waggled her toes in their carpet slippers, to reassure herself she hadn't had a stroke.

Then Rose looked up and rang a taxi firm. In Sheringham. She was getting over her own shock now. Warmth and power seemed to flow into her, from the phone and the voices of the ordinary civilised world outside Wallney.

The taxi firm said someone would be with them in an hour. The man called her "madam" respect-

116

fully. Rose gave Miss Yaxley her arm, and helped her upstairs to pack. Looked out of the broken windows at the garden to avoid seeing the old mottled hands packing the faded grey underwear, and never stopping shaking.

Bastards, thought Rose. They might have *killed* her. They are going to pay for this, no matter what Miss Yaxley says.

She got Miss Yaxley settled back in her chair, with another cup of tea, and her suitcase at her feet. The old lady's colour was better now; the awful greyness was fading. She was beginning to look forward to staying with her sister.

"You need the glazier," said Rose masterfully. "Get those windows done before it rains. Shall I get you one?"

"Yes please!" The old lady looked pathetically grateful.

The glazier was helpful; he would come this afternoon straight away, when Rose explained about "the vandals." But then he, too, was a Sheringham man.

Then Rose asked if she could do some phoning on her own account, and began ringing up hotels asking for accommodations for three people that evening. She had no wish to spend another night in this damned village . . .

But it was Friday; in the height of the holiday season in a big holiday area. Hotel after hotel had nothing. She began to think less bitterly about Philip and the super-efficient Ms. Sampson. It was only after a long search that she got a mere two-star place in Hunstanton that could take them at lunchtime on Saturday. That was it; it was either one more night in that damned village, or go home to Philip with her tail between her legs.

And she would *not* run home to Philip. Well, one more night would not kill them . . . she confirmed the booking at Hunstanton. She heard Miss Yaxley say sharply, "No." But by that time she'd made the booking and rung off.

Miss Yaxley kept on saying no. She must not spend another night in the village. But then the taxi came, and Miss Yaxley was handed into it carefully, tucked up and sent off, Rose reassuring her that she would stay till the glazier came.

The house was very silent, after that. The whole village seemed silent, dreaming under the afternoon sun. Not even a dog was stirring. It was hardly a picture postcard village, even in the sunshine, with its massive poles for phones and power-cables, and the vast blue silos of the farms. But it seemed peaceful enough. Quite a lot of people seemed to be coming and going at the post office, but Friday tended to be shopping day.

But the more peaceful it seemed, the more Rose wanted revenge on it. The telephone lay by her hand, and, in it, power. The power of all the outside world, that could come sweeping in at the touch of a dial, and *drown* Wallney. The world of decent society and standards, of civilised living, of the police and the RSPCA.

And Philip.

She would phone Philip. She looked up the dialling code, and dialled the old familiar number.

And got the old familiar voice of Ms. Sampson.

118

Who enquired politely how the holiday was going, and hoped Rose and the children were enjoying themselves . . .

Rose asked curtly for Philip.

Philip was unfortunately in a meeting. Would she like to leave a message? Was there a number he could ring her back on?

Rose's rage must have crept into her voice. Ms. Sampson asked if there was a problem.

Rose said damn right there was a problem; she should try asking the minister of Cley if there wasn't a problem, and rang off abruptly.

And then thought it would be a good thing to ring the minister of Cley herself.

And got Mrs. minister. The minister was in a meeting. Would she like to leave a message? Was there a number he could ring her back on? Rose hung up more politely that time.

She considered ringing the local police. But a heavy thought told her that probably they'd be unavailable in a meeting too. Anyway, it would be going against poor Miss Yaxley's wishes . . .

Then the glazier turned up, a huge burly man with a red moustache of such splendid length that it joined up with his red sideburns; a jolly man full of jokes and teasing, a very reassuring sort of man who had a mind to bring back flogging for vandals, but at the same time had a lively awareness that vandals meant prosperity for him personally. He measured up the windows for replacement glass, and then cut to size huge sheets of hardboard which he tacked over entire windows. It was a pleasure to make him cups of tea.

It was only when he drove away with a cheery wave that Rose realised it was gone five o'clock, and that her half-hour trip to settle Miss Yaxley's hash had turned into a four-hour mercy mission.

Locking the house, and putting the key in her pocket, she set off through the hated village. Curtain after curtain twitched, but she walked proudly with her nose in the air. If she was being talked about as a witch, at least she would be a witch with style . . .

There were no fewer than three aged men feebly hacking away at the field-hedge as she passed. They got out of her way obligingly enough; but they let her pass without a word.

She found the kids in the kitchen with the cat, looking rather fed up. They'd been untidily at the bread and jam, and left the evidence of their crime for all to see. Obviously they were ceasing to be house-proud. The charm of the house was wearing off for them too, she could tell. Well, at least they would leave tomorrow without a protest; might even be charmed by a wretched two-star dump at Hunstanton.

Except what could they do with the cat, at the two-star dump at Hunstanton? Oh, God, life was so *difficult*. Suddenly, treacherously, Rose was close to tears. She forced them back down with an effort, and said brightly, "Have you had a nice afternoon?"

"Rotten," said Timothy. "We dug for buried treasure."

Suddenly, even in the dimness of the kitchen,

she realised that their shoes were thick with clay, and it was starting to dry and drop off on the kitchen floor.

"What do you mean, buried treasure?" Her treacherous voice jerked suddenly upwards again.

"Like we found in that cupboard this morning," said Jane sulkily.

"Where did you dig?"

"In the garden. Under that stupid rockery."

"What on earth for? What made you think there'd be buried treasure there?" She must keep her patience; they had to amuse themselves *somehow*.

"The cat was scrabbling there. Scrabbling away like mad. So we dug."

"And what did you find?" she asked, all synthetic sweetness and light.

"A rotten old boot."

"A great big boot. We couldn't even get *that* out. It was caught on something. We could get it to waggle, but it wouldn't come out. It must have been caught on something in the ground. But we couldn't find out what. The rockery got in the way . . . so we just left it and covered it up again. It's all right, we left everything tidy," said Timothy. "Don't have a fit, Mum."

It was then that Rose noticed the unpleasant smell in the kitchen. Well, she'd been noticing it for some time. A smell like something really rotting. Like something you'd left in the back of the fridge, when you came back from a month in the Caribbean.

"What's making that smell?" she demanded. "What else have you brought home — a dead rat?"

"*Nothing*, Mum, *honest*."

She followed her sniffing nose round the kitchen, the scent going warmer and colder; like a child seeking out a hidden chocolate Easter egg. Warmer, warmer, colder, warmer, got it!

"Timothy, it's on you. It's all over you. You *stink*! What *have* you been doing? And it's all over you as well, Jane . . . "

"Nothing. Just digging for buried treasure . . . "

"It's on your shoes. And your hands." She pushed him into a chair and hauled off one of his shoes, outraged that her offspring could smell so, for the first time in his life.

The stink of the shoe nearly made her throw up. She threw it into the sink and sluiced water from the pump over it. But the smell just grew worse and worse.

"Sorry," said Tim. "The hole that we dug just got smellier and smellier. We thought it was something Mr. Gotobed had buried from the outhouse. We hardly noticed after a bit, you get used to it. Hey, Mum, where you going?"

She was running, running for her life, for all their lives. For the minister, the police, Philip, anything . . .

"Bolt the door," she shrieked back over her shoulder. "Bolt both the doors. Fasten the windows. Don't answer the door to *anybody*."

*   *   *

Thank God the old men cutting the hedge had gone home for their tea.

She kept well hidden behind the hedge, running crouched up until she made her last burst to the car, keys in her hand. She slammed the car door behind her, pressed down the locking button, turned on the ignition, and the engine roared. Then she let in the clutch . . .

The engine roared again, then stalled. Damn, damn, damn. More haste, less speed. She started the engine again, let in the clutch more gently; the car lurched forward a foot, and the engine stalled again.

It was her panic; she was doing something wrong, and she didn't know what. The car had always started first time, she no longer thought about what you did to start a car. She did it without thinking. Steeling herself with a tremendous effort of will, she slowly turned the ignition again, checked the handbrake was off, let in the clutch with super-human gentleness, got the car slowly moving forward . . .

There was a rough bumping of the wheels; a rough unnatural uneven bumping, a screeching of rubber and metal, and a slight burning smell. There was something wrong, badly wrong, with the bloody car. The screaming engine stalled again. If she went on forcing it, something expensive was going to give.

She looked around the little square. She had been making enough noise to waken the dead. But nothing stirred; there was nothing in sight, not even a dog. Cautiously watching the house doors and street-corners, she opened the car door and peeped down.

All four tires were flat.

One might have been an accident, she thought.

But four was deliberate.

Her magic carpet to civilisation was gone. She bit her lip and whimpered to herself.

She was alone with Wallney.

No, no, the phone. Grabbing her purse and gathering the last remnants of her courage, she ran to the phone-box.

The dangled severed end of the handset mocked her. She did not even waste time going inside.

But she wasn't quite beaten, even then. There was Miss Yaxley's phone. She still had Miss Yaxley's keys in the pocket of her jeans. Her good turn had come back to her aid. They wouldn't have thought of that. She ran faster now than she ever remembered running in her life. Round the corner of the hardboard-blind house she ran, to the back door.

But the back door opened to her push. And hope died. But still she ran to the phone on its little table. Picked it up, hoping against hope.

No dialling tone.

And she sensed, rather than saw, the room darken.

Standing just outside the door were the three old men. Still with their billhooks in their hands. As if they had come to set Miss Yaxley's hedge. In fact one of the old men idly swung at the nearest part of Miss Yaxley's hedge as she watched; and stooped meditatively to pick up the twig that he had sliced off.

She knew that billhook must be razor-sharp; it had cut off a very thin whippy twig.

The old men looked at her. One of them wore spectacles.

"Get you home, missus," he said gently. "Get you home to your children."

Ten

She wondered afterwards why she went home so tamely. Why she didn't take to her heels up the road to Cley, leaving the old men standing. She mightn't be all that fit, but she was a lot fitter than they were, with their wheezing breath and doddering limbs.

But it was their very grandfatherliness that overthrew her. She still thought of the old as being harmless, even calm and wise. Like her own grandfathers had been.

And it was more than that; in their absolute grim surety, grim and righteous as chapel deacons, was the certainty that they had the whole village behind them; a whole society, a whole way of life. If she ran, they would summon younger men with a car, who might not be so gentle. If she was dragged back home panting and struggling and screaming, she would have lost her dignity and more. In their eyes, running away would prove her guilt.

So she went back with them walking behind her.

They were so sure of themselves they did not lay a finger on her.

They all turned in at the garden gate. She looked up, and Timothy and Jane, pale-faced, silent were watching through the open window.

"Wait," said the old man with spectacles. Five yards from her door, she stopped and turned reluctantly. She was so passive that she did not even flinch as the old man raised a fist. She noticed, with some small part of herself that stood coolly aside, that he wore a ring on the third finger of his hand; a ring in which a green stone glinted. She just thought it rather odd that such a grim, dully-dressed old man should wear such a gaudy piece of jewellery. What was he up to? It was all so strange . . .

The next second, he struck her on the forehead. Quite lightly, almost ritually. But there was a small sharp pain, and she knew his ring had cut her. She did not even stagger; just cried out and put her hand to the place and felt blood.

The old man did not put his fist back to his side; he held his hand aloft, again as if in a ritual gesture, to show the others what he had done.

There was a sharp spat from above; a hiss in the air. Then the old man cried out sharply, and they all stared at his upraised hand.

There was a hole in it; a jagged bloody hole through the palm, about half an inch across. Bemused, Rose even saw a glint of blue daylight through it, and a stream of blood running down the old man's wrist, inside the cuff of his thick flannel shirt.

Then the old man doubled up, clenching his hand inside his other hand, and both between his knees.

The other two old men looked up incredulous at the upstairs window, and Rose followed their gaze. Timothy was leaning out, his young face white and set.

"That's for hurting my mother, you old bastard," he said between gritted teeth. "The next time, it'll be your *face*."

From the way he held the long black air-pistol, Rose knew he'd already reloaded. His voice might be trembling, but his hand was rock-steady, and the barrel was pointing straight at the old man's face.

"I'm going to count to five," said Timothy. "One . . . "

But the old men did not run. They stared up at her son. And her son stared back at them, equally implacable.

"Two," said Timothy. "Three. Four . . . "

Heavens, was everybody mad?

She saw his finger tighten on the trigger. Nothing was going to stop him.

The old man raised his hand. The wounded one; it was now red with blood to the fingertips. Rose felt sick.

Then he said, in a voice full of cold quavering hate. "We're going. But we'll be back."

"Then you'll know what to expect," said Timothy, with equal quivering hate.

Then the three old men were shambling out of the gate.

*　　*　　*

Rose walked to the door. She heard the bolts drawn back, with great effort, and Jane pulled her in, her face as white as a sheet. "Mum, you all right?" She shot the bolts again.

"It's only a scratch," said Rose. Then, bewildered, "Where's Tim?"

"Keeping watch," said Jane. "In case the old bastards come back. Sit down. Let me look at that cut."

Rose felt her legs start to give way, and almost fell into a chair. She sat quite still and passive, while her daughter fetched warm water from the kettle, and TCP and Elastoplast from the first aid kit.

"What's happened?" she asked feebly. Meaning what's happened to turn my first-born into almost a murderer?

"We worked it out, Mum," said Jane, with quite amazing calm, and only the slightest tremor in her voice. "That boot we found — it belongs to Sepp Yaxley, doesn't it? He's . . . buried in the garden. They murdered him. Seven years ago, they murdered him. And now they're going to try to murder us."

"Jane, for heaven's sake. This is England. It's not Chicago on the TV . . . "

"So what *are* they going to do with us?" Timothy was now sitting on the top stair, nursing his long black gun with the casual ease of a soldier in Vietnam. "If they let us go, they know we'll only go to the police. And *they'll* come and dig the body up and . . . " He shrugged. "They either have to shut our mouths or . . . " He sounded so coolly excited; as if he were watching a hard-fought football match.

"I don't understand any of it," said Rose, helplessly.

"Oh, I do," said Timothy. "That man who cut you on the forehead. That's because he thought you were a witch. Or he was frightened you might be. He was making sure. He cut you on your forehead to take your witchly powers away. They did that to the witch in *Darkness at Nunmere* on the TV. If you cut a witch above her windpipe, you take all her powers away . . . "

"That's right, Mum," said Jane. "I saw it too."

"But . . . " Rose's voice rose to a wail. "I don't see any of it. I don't see why they killed Sepp Yaxley in the first place. He was their Cunning Man. They *paid* him to do things . . . "

"Show her that account book," said Timothy. He got up from where he was sitting, and she heard him moving softly from room to room upstairs, on the look-out.

Jane came back with the account book, open at the last page. "See," she said. "He must have got across them. They turned against him."

There were only three items on the last page.

> To treating Miss B.R. for the Old
>   Johnnie   Five pounds
> To rail fare to Norwich for the inquest
>   on B.R.   Four pounds
> To rail fare to Norwich to hear the
>   verdict   Four pounds

Jane said softly, "They must have blamed him for her death. Nobody came to see him after that. Nobody paid him anything."

Rose looked at the last date. It was the 25th of May, 1981.

"But . . . but . . . " said poor Rose.

"Oh, don't tell us this is England, Mum. Or the twentieth century or anything. The last Cunning Man was only done in in 1945. He was a farm-worker in the Cotswolds. They found him dead with a pitchfork through him. We saw it on a pro-gramme about Fabian of the Yard — you know, the famous Flying Squad detective. Fabian inves-tigated it for years — he even went back to the village dozens of times after he retired. He knew it was a ritual killing — there was no other motive. He always believed it was witchcraft. But he never got anywhere. He reckoned the whole village was in the murder together — that they appointed one man to do the killing, and they weren't saying any-thing. You can't get anywhere if a whole village is against you."

It was the matter-of-fact way she said it that chilled Rose. She wished profoundly that she'd taken more care in controlling what they watched on TV. But when they both had portables in their own rooms . . .

Timothy had resumed his seat at the top of the stairs. He said, a little pityingly Rose thought, "How did they catch you, Mum? Had they duffed in the car?"

Rose nodded mutely.

"And duffed in the phone-box?"

She nodded again.

"What about Miss Yaxley?"

Humbly, she told him. It was very strange, having your son boss you about with such certainty. He was suddenly very like Philip; they were both suddenly very like Philip. Well, it's better than being soft and helpless like me, she thought. And hopelessly wished Philip were here.

"Point is, what happens now?" said Timothy. "I don't reckon they'll try anything before dark. They know what they'll get."

"You *wouldn't* shoot them in the face, would you, Tim?"

"Damn right I would. They're going to kill us."

"Oh, that's *silly*. How could they? Daddy knows where we are. Miss Yaxley knows we're here. The minister of Cley knows we're here. They'd never get away with it. Daddy would raise heaven and earth. The police wouldn't rest. And if they found our bodies, or even us just missing . . . "

"That's what *you* think! We've worked out one perfect way they could do it already. Tie us up in bed upstairs, and set fire to the whole cottage. With all these oil-lamps and a cat roving the house . . . whole families die in accidental fires every week. You see it on the local TV. It doesn't even make the main news headlines."

"But the police would find the ropes tying us . . . "

"They'd be lucky to find anything of us. How could they even get a fire-engine up this path? And where would it come from? Cromer? Sheringham?

Place would be a pile of smouldering ashes by the time they even got here. I mean, they wouldn't even know the house was burning, unless they saw the light in the sky from Cley. And this is the time they burn the stubble anyway. I can see one field of stubble burning from here. Between us and Cley."

Poor Rose could find nothing to say.

"Point is," said Timothy, "we've got to save ourselves. I can hold them off till dark, because I've scared them now. They'll be looking at that old bastard's hand, and wondering what it's like having the same hole in your face. But after dark, one petrol-bomb through a downstairs window . . . "

"Can't we make a run for it?" asked Jane.

"They're watching the house. Pretending to be cutting the hedges. I can see five of them. They're all round . . . "

This just isn't *happening*, thought Rose wildly.

"One of us might get away, around dusk," said Tim thoughtfully. "If one of us got away, they wouldn't dare harm the others. Not unless the one that got away was caught. Where's the nearest help, Mum, d'you think?"

"The minister," said Rose weakly. "The minister at Cley. He knows . . . most of it, anyway. He wanted to help us get out this morning. He offered . . . "

"Pity you didn't take his advice," said Timothy, mercilessly.

"Or the police," said Rose.

"They'll be keeping an eye on the police-station," said Timothy. "On the whole Cley road.

133

You'll have to work across the fields, Jane. Or go down to the shore and along the beach. They might even send someone down to the beach. Keep to the hedgerows, that's best."

"Jane can't go!" said Rose desperately.

"Well I can't go," said Tim. "Jane's useless with the pistol. Can't hit *anything*." Then he added, "And you're too big, Mum." Then he added, in a kinder voice, "Besides, you've got to stay and talk to them, if they come back."

It began to rain towards dusk. Great clouds swept in over the sea, and the dusk began to come terribly quickly. Rose just sat, without volition, without belief. All the life seemed to have run out of her.

She started out of a cold doze, as Timothy spoke to her. Kindly. Reassuringly. Just like Philip. She looked at her son. He looked tense, but in a way he was loving it. She remembered an army colonel talking on the radio once. Young men make the best soldiers, he had said. Eighteen-year-olds, even sixteen-year-olds, make the best killers. They have no imagination; they do not understand what it is to inflict or suffer pain and death. How about thirteen-year-olds? she thought wildly. She had read of thirteen-year-olds committing murder. In America even ten- or eleven-year-olds. With guns. It was all a video game to them, at that age.

Mature people make the worst killers, the colonel had said. Because they can empathize with pain. My God, she thought, I am a useless quivering mass of empathy.

"Got a little job for you, Mum. Now listen! All I want is for you to go down to the outhouse. Use it, if you like. You must be bursting by now. But the thing is, when you come out, forget to close the outhouse door. Just leave it open, about a foot or so. Right? Now can you remember that? Don't close the door afterwards. Just leave it open, carelessly. *Open*, right?"

Wearily, she nodded. There seemed no harm in leaving an outhouse door open.

"Off you go, then!" He hauled her out of her chair and gave her a helpful push towards the door.

"Put your anorak hood up," said Tim. "It's *raining*. You'll get your hair wet."

Without thought, she let him push it up for her; he patted her hair back in place with affection, and let her pass.

It seemed a long lonely walk to the outhouse. She glanced about, nervously. She spotted one man cutting a hedge at a distance. He straightened up as she emerged. Watched her all the way to the outhouse door. It was strangely humiliating. She pulled the door hard shut, and bolted it on the inside.

The need to go came on excruciatingly; she only just got her jeans down in time. Even her body felt a hostile stranger.

Afterwards, she nearly shut the door behind her. From sheer habit. It was only the sight of Tim's

135

anxious face and gesturing hand in the kitchen window that reminded her in time.

She walked back to the garden, in a cold sweat. Couldn't she do *anything* right, even something as simple as leaving an outhouse door open?

"Well done," said Tim warmly. "Good old Mum." He gave her a comforting kiss, and she nearly wept.

He had stopped her from closing the back door either. And she noticed he was now wearing his dark sweater and dark trousers, and had soot smeared across his face.

"Right," he said. "You start lighting the oil-lamps. Keep them as near the windows as possible. Kitchen first. That'll give the bastards something to watch."

She went to the kitchen windowsill where the oil-lamps were kept. Began taking off shades and chimneys, with quivering hands. Then struck a match and went along the row, lighting them one after the other.

"Is that right?" she asked humbly.

But her son was no longer there. Startled, she looked around. "Tim?"

"Shush," said Jane. "He's wriggling down the hedge. Don't *look*, Mum, for hell's sake." Then she added, "Good, he's made it."

"What's he *doing*?" Rose felt her panic rise again.

"You know the outhouse," said Jane. "Well, when Mr. Gotobed came to see to us, he didn't carry it out through the garden, where it might offend us. He took it out of the outhouse through a hatch in the back wall. Which leads straight out into the next field. If Tim can get the hatch open, one of us can get out that way. Into the hedge."

Jane was putting on Tim's red anorak now, over the top of her own blue one. Zipping it up, pulling up the hood so it hid her face completely.

She looked out of the dimming window.

"There's Tim signalling. Time to go. Bye-bye, Mum. Love you."

And then she was strolling down the garden, giving nervous looks around, in Tim's anorak.

The outhouse door closed behind her.

Rose waited for she knew not what. Then a figure in a red anorak was coming up the path, head down and hood up against the rain.

"Jane?"

The door closed behind the figure. The hood was pushed back, and the grinning face of Tim appeared.

"She's away through the hatch, Mum. Into the hedge and on her way. It'll take her a couple of hours, but they won't get her now. It's getting dark, and she's the best hider I know. I blacked her face and closed the hatch, so they won't spot anything. All we have to do now is wait."

Eleven

They waited till it was very nearly dark. Half an
hour had passed, without a sign or shout from the
outside. Jane must be well away by this time. Head-
ing for the minister, the police, civilisation. It was
a warming thought, and she hugged it to herself.
Whatever happened through this dreadful night,
her daughter was safe.

She was at the upstairs back window, keeping
watch, while Tim kept watch at the front. There
was still a little pink light in the sky to the west;
the last of day. The last of any day she might ever
see. She shivered and hugged her anorak round
her; but she still could not quite make herself believe that anybody was going to kill anybody.
Oddly it was still the villagers' power to kill she
doubted. Not Tim's. Tim was lost, quietly exalted
in some dream of war. Every upstairs window was
wide open. There was a little neat shining row of
air-pistol slugs arranged along every windowsill in

the house. Carefully spaced an inch apart, for speedy picking up. All the movies had come home to Tim. *Dirty Harry, Lethal Weapon II, Full Metal Jacket, Rambo, The Exterminator.* Barred from the cinema, forbidden them at home, Tim had watched them all at friends' houses. Over and over. They had started their graduation in killing a year early . . .

"Mum?" Tim's voice was low and urgent, but not at all panicky. "Mum, they're coming. About four of them. Come and hold the torch for me. Don't switch it on till they're really close, and then let them have it full in the face. It'll blind them."

She took the big torch from him; aware that her hands were shaking, and that his hand was merely . . . tensed, thrumming.

"Don't stand right in the window, Mum!" Mild exasperation had crept into his tone. "Stand to one side, so they can't see you." He himself was standing next to the window, back to the wall, gun pointing upwards gracefully, professionally. How often had she seen that pose on TV? *Cagney and Lacey, Dempsey and Makepiece, Miami Vice* . . . It was more familiar than the England team lining up in a defensive wall for a free kick, more familiar than Graham Gooch adjusting his helmet . . .

She heard the footsteps crunching up the path from the sea; crunching on the old bricks by the gate.

"Right, Mum, *now.*"

She flicked on the torch. In its white glare, she saw every detail of Mr. Gotobed's laid hedge, the straggling rose-trees that he had freed from the

139

weeds, so long ago. Four men in old shabby coats with white faces, and hands reaching up to shield their eyes from the light . . .

"That's far enough," shouted Tim. His voice rose, not with hysteria. But with pressure; like a pressure-gauge mounting in some disaster movie. He was very close to firing . . .

The men stopped abruptly; perhaps they could hear the tone in his voice too. Then the one with the spectacles, the one with the bandaged hand, called out, "Missus, we got your daughter, hare."

And Jane was pushed forward from the back. It was quite clearly Jane. Her blue anorak was very dirty; and she looked pretty scared.

"She shouldn't be wandering around the country after dark," said another of the men.

And somebody snickered. It was a horrible sound, that filled Rose with despair.

"We don't want to do her no harm," said the man in the spectacles. "Just hurry up and open that door, so she can come on in."

Rose saw they were keeping a very tight grip on her, one on either side.

"C'mon, missus, open that door . . . "

What else was there to do?

And then she saw a movement on the ground, nearer the house. A small cautious furtive movement, that wavered at the edge of her flicking torchlight.

And then the cat stepped into the circle of light. Yaxley's cat.

It walked up to the men, to within two yards of them.

It inspected them, with a certain curiosity, a pricking of its dark ears.

They saw it. At least someone did.

"That's Sepp's cat," said someone uneasily. The men seemed to edge a little closer to each other.

The cat looked at one face after another. It seemed to take its time. One, two, three.

And then, before Rose could blink, it launched itself at the fourth face; the man with the spectacles. There was a wild scream.

"My eyes. Gerrit off, gerrit off."

There was a milling mass of arms around the cat. And at the same moment, Jane broke free and ran off round the house.

"Back door, Mum, back door, quick," shouted Tim.

Behind her, as she ran downstairs, she heard the hissing chug of Tim's air-pistol and a man shouting, "Christ, my face. Christ, my face."

Then the back door was open and bolted again, and Rose's sobbing daughter was in her arms.

And immediately, Tim was yelling for them upstairs.

But when they got there and shone the torch, the garden was empty. But for the stretched-out body of Yaxley's cat. And a pair of spectacles, that glinted. But only one lens glinted. The other had some stuff on it.

Tim did a careful round of the other windows. "Put out the oil-lamps downstairs, Mum." he called. "We don't want to make their job easy for them."

Rose did as she was told and returned. Jane had stopped crying already.

"They caught me on the beach," she said, bitterly. "Only I got fed up with crawling through hedges . . . "

"Stupid nerd," said Timothy. "You might have known. I warned you."

"You try crawling through hedges . . . "

Rose comforted herself that nothing serious could have happened to Jane. She looked sadly down at the body of the cat.

"It knew," said Timothy.

"Knew what?"

"Knew who the real murderer was. It just looked at the other three, then went for him. The cat must have seen it all happen. It remembered. Cats never forget anything. Well, it had its revenge. Nearly clawed his face to bits. I bet he hasn't got much to look out of now . . . "

"*Timothy*!" From somewhere, Rose still had the power to be shocked.

Tim shrugged, and pretended to draw a bead at the old garden gate. "They'll be a bit sorry for themselves for a while now. They were flailing at the cat with their billhooks and hitting each other. And I hit one of them in the cheek, I think. That'll have knocked a few teeth out. And with what the cat did . . . they won't be back for half an hour, I reckon." He sighed. "But they'll have the young blokes with them, the next time."

They did.

They were standing in huddles in the lane, behind the hedge. They were standing in huddles all round the back garden. The sound of their excited muttering, their arguments and plans came up like the sound of a disturbed hive of bees.

Tim had done his best. Getting Jane to suddenly shine the torch on a bit of hedge, from one window after another, making them duck before the air-pistol chugged and another slug went whining away.

But there were no more yelps; no sign that he had hit anything else. And they had bottles with rags in the top; she had seen their glint in the light of the torch.

Rose sat in her daze; she no longer had the heart; she despaired. She was just glad the children had something to occupy themselves in their last moments; that they were still fighting and not afraid. Oddly, she was proud of them. Philip would have been proud of them too . . .

She thought sadly of Philip; of what he would have to face when he came. But she thought he would survive it, somehow. Make a new life for himself, eventually . . . perhaps the minister could help him. Perhaps Philip would work like hell to put two and two together, drive the police frantic with the power he had in the company and his important friends. Philip might even prove murder, have revenge.

But what good was revenge? She and the kids would all be . . .

"I think they're going to have a go, Mum," said Timothy, quietly. "They're getting all worked up to it." Then he added in disgust, "Half of them are drunk."

He was ever his father's son. No time for the peasants of this world. He probably would kill one of them, before the flames got too high. Maybe more than one.

Well, he was entitled.

Then she heard him say, startled.

"Hey, what's *that*?"

She ran to the window.

A pair of searchlights, up towards Wallney. Little searchlights that were nearly parallel to the ground, but bobbed and swayed upwards, uncertainly.

A car, forcing its way up the old path from the village. She could hear its heavy engine now, and the smashing of branches. Some other aid to killing them?

But the faces in the lane had turned to watch the lights come. And they stood very still; not like men who are welcoming support. They stood with their arms flaccid by their sides; suddenly for some reason no longer wary even of the danger of the air-pistol. Something had made them quite forget about the danger of the air-pistol . . .

The saving headlights got nearer; the throb of the diesel engine louder, the crashing of the branches more frantic. And now there were blue lights, revolving and winking above the headlights. The red legend

STOP POLICE

It stopped about fifty yards away, its headlights lighting up everything. And under the brilliance of

144

those lights, the crowd in the lane began to . . . melt, dribble away, vanish.

"That won't save them," said Tim with great satisfaction. "They can run as far as they like. I recognised half of them. The woman from the mini-market was there. *And* her husband."

Rose shuddered at his tone; there wasn't the slightest trace of mercy in it. Everyone was going to pay to the uttermost penny.

But it was time to welcome their saviours, who were getting out of the white, striped Range Rover, and walking along the path to the cottage. Two policemen, with white covers to their caps; one without a white cover, and a bare-headed man in the middle. She strained her eyes to make out who it was; but the figure was in silhouette against the headlights.

It was too short and squat for Philip; too broad for the little minister. Certainly never Miss Yaxley . . . who *was* it?

The figure stopped at the gate and turned, lifting its face to the upstairs window.

It had black spectacles; mended on the bridge with black adhesive tape. It wore dirty rubbers.

"You all right, missus?" shouted Mr. Gotobed. She shouted yes.

"That's good. Wiv had one killin'. We don't want no more."

"They killed the cat," she shouted. "It's lying in the front garden."

Tim shone his torch, at where the body lay.

But there was no body; there wasn't even any blood. Of Yaxley's cat, there was no sign.

They spent the night at the police station in Sheringham. They spent the night, but they didn't sleep. Philip was there before midnight; hurling his weight about with the police. The little minister was there, desperately concerned, trying to help. And policemen asking questions and telephoning. And Jane, now it was all over, keeping on rushing off to be sick. And Timothy, telling all he knew, consigning people to custody without blinking an eye.

"And there was a tall thin bloke with reddish hair cut very short — I've seen him in the post office. He drives a tractor — a Fordson tractor — I can't remember the number-plates. I think he'd got a tattoo on his left wrist . . . " Tim demonic, tireless, sipping endless cans of Coke and damning souls to hell. The avenging angel. He frightened her now, more than the old man with the spectacles had frightened her. And Jane, at his shoulder, backing him up between her bouts of sickness, nodding at every word he said. Every power of the state at his command; the perks of the rich. And Philip standing watching him, approving, equally avenging, equally merciless.

She could almost feel sorry for the villagers she saw being led past the police station's swinging doors. Shrunken, baffled, hopeless. Ripped out of their tiny cosy world into a huge world that wanted only their names and addresses and their confessions and their punishment.

Rose felt more alone than she ever had in her life.

The little minister came across to her, and put an arm round her and unashamedly held her hand.

"Oh, Father," she said. "Is there no mercy anywhere?"

"Yes, there is mercy," he said, nodding wearily.

She hoped he wasn't going to talk about God; try to stick God over every wound like a sticking plaster.

And he didn't let her down.

"In Mr. Gotobed," he said.

Then added, "And in you yourself, my dear."

About the Author

Robert Westall is a renowned author of books for adults and young adults and is the recipient of two Carnegie Medals, the Guardian Award, and a Smarties Prize in his native England where he makes his home.

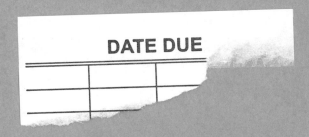

DATE DUE